ROGUES AND RAJAS

Dark Tales for Tumultuous Times

SV Iyer is a scientist by training and a publisher by profession. Previously editor-in-chief at Knowello, a business and finance platform, and managing editor at Jaico Publishing House, Iyer has embarked on journeys from Bollywood to Belgium in a quest for exceptional content, innovative concepts and gifted authors. Hailing from Kanyakumari and currently residing in vibrant Mumbai, Iyer pursues writing for a livelihood, dabbles in anthropology for leisure, and avidly gathers rare narratives of trade and warfare along the Indian coast.

ROGUES AND RAJAS

Dark Tales for Tumultuous Times

SV IYER

Illustrations by Anjana Sridharan

hachette
INDIA

First published in 2023 by Hachette India
(Registered name: Hachette Book Publishing India Pvt. Ltd)
An Hachette UK company
www.hachetteindia.com

1

ISBN 978-93-5731-262-2

For sale in the Indian Subcontinent only

Hachette Book Publishing India Pvt. Ltd
4th & 5th Floors, Corporate Centre
Plot No. 94, Sector 44, Gurugram – 122003, India

Typeset by Manmohan Kumar, Delhi

Printed and bound in India
by Manipal Technologies Limited

FSC
www.fsc.org
MIX
Paper from
responsible sources
FSC™ C043100

To Amma and Appa,
for their unconditional love

CONTENTS

Preface ix

1. The Stonemasons of Suchindram 1
2. The Chola with the Charred Leg 17
3. The Death of Chanakya 30
4. Kingmaker and King 49
5. Chandashoka Breaks Out of Hell 64
6. Gunadhya and the Book of Blood 77
7. Beauty and the Beast of Bengal 90
8. Foreign Ships in Lanka 100
9. Didda and the Crown of Kashmir 115
10. The Lost Treasure of Bimbisara 131
11. The Favourite Son and the Other One 142
12. Winner Takes All 157
13. The Indomitable Gaur 172
14. The Trouble with Twin Kings 184
15. Alexander Gets a Guru 202

Acknowledgements 216

PREFACE
A STRUGGLE TO STAY WITHIN THE LINES

The air smelled fresh and damp. Across the open window, crystal-winged damselflies sliced soft threads of sunlight into rainbow sprays. The author watched in a daze as they winked in and out of the frame. In the muddled time, the light seemed to coalesce on the sill, and a large glass jar came into view.

Woah! How did that get here? Was it always there?

The author's spectacled eyes drew up like giant wheels against the jar and peered into it. It was clean and empty. Then, a knock sounded against the lid. It came from *inside* the jar.

But there's nothing in it! I can see clear through it to the garden outside.

Again, the knocking.

The author unscrewed the jar and nearly had a heart attack: a tiny, perfectly formed girl climbed out. She had four arms. In one, she carried a book. With the other three, she reached into the jar and pulled out a beautiful brown-and-gold veena.

'What? Who? What!' came the blubbering questions. 'Wait. Is that… are you… Thumbelina?'

The pixie rolled her eyes and said, 'Recognize me well; I am your inspiration!'

The author measured the girl between forefinger and thumb, and replied sadly, 'My inspiration is small. No wonder my pages are still blank.'

'Size doesn't matter,' consoled the muse. 'Just start pushing the keys and you will see what miracles I create. Your head is already buzzing with ancient voices. What do you say?'

'They are stubborn. The stencil of history is before me, but the voices insist on breaking the mould.'

The muse strummed her veena lightly as if measuring notes for a new composition. 'Never fear, I am here to keep them in check. They will not stray too far from the line.'

Her music, the author noticed, seemed less classical, more fusion. Would this spontaneous little creature stick to history as the old books gave it?

'You know,' she said, 'it is conventional to start with a prayer.'

The author sent a fervent plea to the Goddess – and began tapping at the keys.

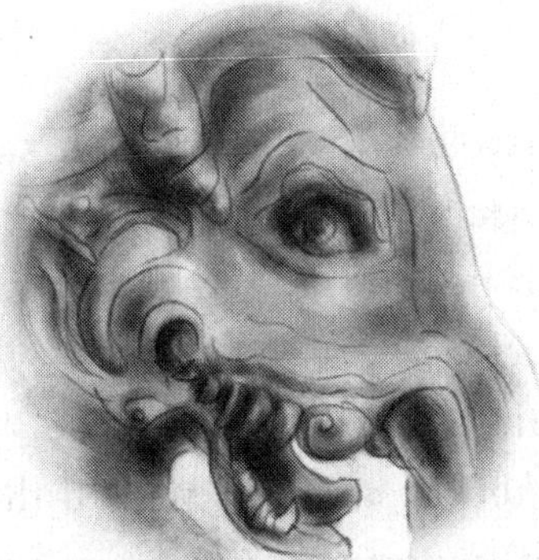

THE STONEMASONS OF SUCHINDRAM

The king was concluding a morning briefing with his advisers.

A balding minister, ash and *chandan* crumbling from his forehead on to his over-large nose, stepped forward. The king nodded at him.

'Sire,' said the minister, 'there is the matter of the temple in Suchindram.'

The king waved at him to go on.

'Since the last bulletin from the priests, the builders have enclosed the main shrine behind gold doors. As you know, sire, the temple is now a vast, granite labyrinth of pillared halls, spacious corridors, open courtyards and artificial hills.'

The king stroked his beard with satisfaction. The temple would secure his legacy for generations to come. Every day, the people praised him for raising such a wondrous structure.

'What remains to be done?' he asked.

'Why… *nothing at all,* sire!' replied the oily flatterer. 'The temple is imposing, mysterious and magnificent. Simply entering its bell-encrusted doorway brings one into the presence of divinity.'

A hemming from behind caused the minister and others to turn around. The king's poet had entered the room and stood smiling by the door. His eyes were dancing, and the ruler guessed that he was about to be entertained.

'You have something to add, glib one?' questioned the king.

'Why, it's… *nothing at all, sire,*' the man mimicked, mincing forwards. The minister flushed as murmurs and sniggers rippled through the room.

'Nothing at all. To be precise, you have a barren, cheerless temple that is nothing at all.'

'Speak with care!' warned the king.

'I'd cut off my tongue before it offends you!' replied the poet at once. 'This careless fool has brought you a rare gift, sire. Be pleased to view it and forgive my frivolous words. I may add that the gift is someone else's and I am merely the courier.'

So saying, he whisked out a figurine from the manifold pleats of his robes and held it forth for all to see. A gasp went up in the room. In measured steps, he walked forwards and set it before the king.

The figurine resembled the dancing Shiva, the Nataraja. Only, he was dancing on his hands. Framed in an arch of carved flames, the divine acrobat balanced on one palm. His other hand formed a *mudra,* a third hand raised a flame, and a fourth held a drum. His clothes and ornaments whirled askew, as he somersaulted gracefully below the arch. His face was fierce, moustached and intensely focused.

No one spoke. It was as if they waited for that magnificent figure to finish his fantastic dance. His power over them was complete.

'Is it possible this is made of *stone*?' sighed one of the men in admiration, 'It looks as if it's moving!'

'It must be a trick of the light,' said another. 'Some mechanical secret, perhaps? Or something added to the stone.' Murmurs of agreement and delight echoed in the room.

'Poet, who created this?'

'Sire, word of your grand temple has spread to all corners of the land. Men from everywhere are vying to participate in its construction. Three stonemasons, newly arrived and residing on the outskirts of the city, are responsible for this piece. Should you allow it, they will carve such tremendous figurines from plain granite that the gods might take the temple for heaven itself!

'Majesty, think what tales could be carved on to those bland pillars. What lamp-bearing beauties could light your way down its long, dark passages. What fierce guardians would adorn the gateways and arches. These gifted men were born to complete your temple! Then might the minister more truly say that nothing at all remains to be done.'

The kings listened to every word, not once taking his eyes off the Nataraja. There was no doubt in his mind that the stonemasons would work on his temple. But how could he inspire them to perform their best, to create an *unparalleled* masterpiece?

'Invite the stonemasons to work on the temple,' he said. 'Speak to them thus: carve us your most terrifying, most intricate, most inspired visions. Carve such wonders as have never been seen before and as none may mimic hereafter. Whatever is the weight of the dust that falls from your carvings, we will equal its weight in gold as your reward!'

The room broke out in shouts of praise for the king. The poet bowed with a sense of personal triumph and left to carry out his master's commands.

The three stonemasons went to work. Over many months, they gave form to startling, dreamlike creatures in the temple. Doorways sprouted ram-horned, bulbous-eyed dragons; ceilings and passageways began to mirror each other with geometric strips; stories of heroes and damsels climbed up the pillars scene by scene, cascading into domes over gates and halls; and unimaginable deities took root in dark nooks.

One week, they found an army of fierce *yali*s carved around a courtyard. Part lion, part horse, the gigantic creatures reared up on their hoofs and bared their fanged maws at passers-by. Like little boys, some of the priests surreptitiously climbed up and put their hand into the granite mouths, to feel the curious thrill of *almost* having it bitten off.

Another week, the dark northern corridor became an avenue of a hundred shapely, doe-eyed *apsaras*. Intricately ornamented in rock-cut girdles, anklets, earrings and necklaces, each held a granite oil lamp in her hands. When lit, the lamps cast mysterious shadows over the soft figures.

While the priests went about their business, admiring the new works, it was understood that none must disturb the sculptors at their job.

In one of the courtyards, the stonemasons were busy carving an avatar of Shiva. One worked to create twenty-six faces in a five-tiered pyramid. Another chipped away rock to form fifty-two arms and all the weapons a god of destruction could want. Stone dust piled steadily at their feet, covering their knees, hands and face in a fine sheen.

The third, who carved the mountain on which the god sat, made smooth, tumid boulders. *Not so intricate, this,* he thought. *Not much dust will come off it... and that means, less gold for us.*

His attention wandered to the scatterings of chips and flakes visible through the haze of half-floating powder by their feet. *How much dust will we collect,* he wondered. *How much gold will there finally be?*

And then a doubt that had been nagging him for a while surfaced.

Will the king really give us gold dust in equal measure to the stone dust we produce, he wondered. *There is so much dust! Will he really part with such a vast amount of gold? What if he changes his mind and gives us only a fraction of it?*

The thought swam round and round in his head. Before he realized it, the block of stone he was working on had all turned to dust! He looked at the pile thoughtfully. Nothing of a statue had been created, so he shouldn't really be paid for this dust.

But what if he did add it to the pile? Who would know? An idea began to take shape in his mind.

If the king cheated them and gave them only a part of the dust's weight in gold, he deserved to be cheated in return. And if the king kept his word? Why, then the three of them would simply be that much richer!

Temptation, like a slow-furling creeper, took insidious hold of the stonemason. He picked up a fresh block of stone and began carving.

An hour later, his companion shouted down from his perch.

'Hey, you! Pay attention there. That's the fifth piece you've reduced to rubble!'

'Oh,' replied the man sheepishly. 'Yes. That is, I'm afraid I have… I seem to have done so. Well, it's just a piece of rock after all.'

The second stonemason's jaw dropped. 'Just a piece of…! Are you unwell or something?'

The third stonemason, who was sitting much higher up the wall to carve faces, sneezed. He blew his nose on his dhoti and climbed down.

'I heard that!' he said. 'What's going on with you? Just because you're working in a Shiva temple doesn't mean you get to destroy all our creations!'

'All right, all right. Just hear me out first. It's just... have you thought about our reward?'

'Thought about it! All that gold. Who wouldn't?' said the second stonemason.

'Right? I dream about it every night!' said the third one.

'Then you are sure that the king will keep his word?'

The men paused and looked at each other.

'Well, now that you mention it, I have been a little worried... After all, this temple is so large. Even the king – could he have enough gold to match so much dust?'

'Don't be fools, brothers. He is the king. He gave his word publicly. He must keep it or lose all dignity as a ruler.'

'You're the fool! We all know rulers have a way of making lavish promises when they need us, only to wriggle out once they've got their way.'

'The local heads might do so, but surely The Head would not. Would he? Would he destroy his reputation on so small a matter?'

'Oh, you are a naïve fool! He is the all-powerful ruler of the land. He could point to the afternoon sun and say how cool the moonlit night is... and not even his mighty ministers and military chiefs would dare contradict him. What could three small men do to his reputation? We are to him as this stone is to us – easily reduced to rubble.'

'Then, what is to be done? We have put our souls into these creations. Must we be cheated like this?'

The first stonemason waded into a mound of dust and began kicking it hither and thither. 'Even this humble dust could bury a king if there was enough of it,' he shouted gleefully. 'Let us create more dust, *more dust*! And let the king match what he can!'

'Hush, hush!' cried the others and dragged him back. 'These granite walls echo, and someone may hear!'

'All right!' he muttered, shrugging them off. 'But are we agreed?'

His companions looked uneasily at each other. 'What if the king does mean to keep his word?'

'What if he does?' the first stonemason said truculently. 'His kind have stolen from us for generations. Where does all their wealth come from, do you think? Ministers tax our honest earnings, strongmen extort bribes, armies take our rations, even priests demand offerings these days. We toil and toil, and for what? When is it our turn to enjoy the fruit of our labour?'

'He is right,' the second stonemason said, turning to the third one. 'This is our chance. We must be realistic about it.'

'All right,' his fellow worker replied, giving in. 'Then let us be realistic about it. Turning five blocks to rubble like that is foolish. You will have a pile of dust as high as the *gopuram*. We do this: for every fistful of dust that falls from our carvings, we will add an extra fistful. Agreed?'

The others nodded.

Unperceived by them, the king's spy heard their conversation and reported it to his master.

In time, the temple stood complete. It was magnificent beyond words!

A great ceremony was held and the king himself took part in worshipping the presiding deity. All who entered the premises oohed and aahed at the endless wonders.

The gifted carvers had turned the coarse rock into divine beings, revealing captivating dancers from heaven and muscular beasts from myth. Fierce warriors from China and Persia were sculpted with their armours and habits. There was even a musical miracle, created with an arrangement of long, bone-slender pillars that, when struck, produced celestial harmony.

In the days that followed, it seemed the people were infused with a new-found devotion, for they turned up frequently at the temple. The priests were delighted.

Eventually, the three stonemasons were summoned to the palace.

They were escorted to an arena specially built for the purpose of feting the talented masons. This structure was narrower at the bottom and high-walled. Beyond it, and well above the wall, benches had been set up on high wooden frames, so anyone sitting there would have a clear view of what went on down in the centre. Throngs of men, women and children filled the seats, anticipating the arrival of the stonemasons and the festivities that would follow.

As the three luminaries walked into the strange bowl, great shouts of 'bravo!' and 'well done!' rent the air. The stonemasons bowed this way and that, beaming with pride.

Finally, the master of ceremonies stood up to speak and a hush fell over the grounds.

'Citizens! The great temple is an unparalleled creation. It rivals the genius of Vishvakarma himself. Over these years, you have all witnessed the prodigious talent of the three masters who stand before us. Though they were not born of this land, their names will forever more be first among the best of us.'

The master paused as the crowds cheered. He then resumed.

'You three stonemasons: you were promised gold dust in a measure equal to the dust that fell from your stone while you created statues for the temple. In recognition of your distinguished service, the full reward shall now be bestowed upon you. Bring in the gold!'

As the people watched, a gargantuan gate opened and brightly decked elephants paraded into the arena. Giant sacks were tied to their back and legs. As the beasts began perambulating the field, someone slit the sacks open and gold dust spilled out. The elephants continued walking and the ground became carpeted in layer upon layer of gold.

The crowds groaned in awe and envy at the fabulous sight. The stonemasons looked on, mesmerized. The elephants marched round and round the arena and gold sand piled up in circuit. The elephants walked and walked, the circles got shorter and shorter and the pile grew higher and higher.

The cheering ceased. The whisper of a gentle breeze could be heard and the relentless crunching of elephant feet upon glittering grains of fine metal.

Whatever will they do with so much gold? someone in the crowd murmured.

How will they cart it all away? someone else said.

Why, it has almost reached their heads! You can barely see the men anymore.

At the moment, the sacks on the elephants' legs ran out and their mahouts led them out. A collective sigh gave witness to the surge of relief that rolled over the people. The master of ceremonies stood up.

'Good stonemasons, this gold that you see is in equal measure to the dust that piled up from your carvings.'

The masons looked somewhat taken aback for standing in such a deep well of gold. It came up to their foreheads. The cheers of the people were muted from where they stood. Still, they noticed when the crowd suddenly fell silent. They heard the gates open and then, once more, the crunching of elephant feet and the sweeping sound of gold grains falling out.

Sweat ran down their brows.

'Should we climb up a bit perhaps,' one of them whispered to the other.

'What if the elephant crushes you,' came the reply, as his companion stood on tiptoe and eyed the smooth nails of a giant foot that passed by, level to his eye.

The master of ceremonies could be heard speaking.

'Citizens! Hear the words of our king. You see before you three men who are gifted with great skill. A talent that we say rivals that of the

gods' own architect. We have honoured and rewarded them. Would that the gods had given them honour in equal measure to skill. For you see before you, citizens, three men who have cheated our kingdom.

'The gold grains that now fall upon their heads are the measure of their greed, which enticed them to add an extra fistful of dust to every fistful that rightfully fell from their work. Even so, our king keeps his word and will pay in full the quantity that was billed to him.'

A rumbling greeted these words as cries of *Thieves! Crooks!* and many curses fell upon the three.

'You three stonemasons: you have been found guilty of deceiving king and country. You knowingly and despicably cheated the nation out of its gold. Such greedy, contemptible men should not be associated with the work of the lord. Your names will be struck from the record and never again mentioned. No one shall know who carved the great temple of Suchindram.

'Furthermore, since your love of gold led you to this state, it is the decision of the court that you shall remain with it for all time.'

The stonemasons shrieked, but no one heard their cries in the furore above. People stamped their feet and spat in their direction.

The elephants walked on and on, scattering gold all around. The men scrambled up, slipping and sliding against the grains, but the great beasts kept them hemmed in. In the end, when the sacks ran out a second time, the men were buried tightly to their necks. Under the hot sun, the metal heated and burned their flesh. The crowds watched in horrified fascination until a monstrous war elephant was sent in. The beast walked over the men's head, bursting them apart like ripe pumpkins, silencing them once and for all.

♦•♦•♦•♦•♦•♦•♦

The moon had set, but there was no sign of dawn yet. The minister was making his way to the temple tank for his morning rituals. As he passed the western door of the temple, he saw a dull glow of light. It silhouetted a group of people crouching by the wall. Wary but curious, he walked up softly behind them.

A man was carving something on the lowest part of the wall by the door. Another held up a lamp so the carver could see clearly. Behind the pair, another man stood watching in silence. He was guarded by two spear-bearers on either side.

As the lamp shifted in the night breeze, its light revealed the central figure to be the court poet.

'What is happening here?' asked the minister.

The bodyguards came to attention immediately. Unfazed, the poet peered into the gloaming and recognized the minister. He beckoned the man forward.

Spears were lowered and the minister came closer. He bent down to the see a simple but deep carving on the wall near the ground. It showed three human heads in a row. A fierce elephant towered over them with its feet raised to deliver the fatal blow.

'They will not be completely forgotten after all. It is the king's final mercy,' sighed the poet.

THE CHOLA WITH THE CHARRED LEG

Vennil Kuyathiyar, poet and friend to the king, scratched his nose with the back of his quill, then scratched at the parchment before him:

The sovereign arrived in splendour on a magnificent tusker [*he wrote*], with row upon row of armour-clad troops to escort him through the capital. All down the streets, the people cheered to see their young ruler: his unclouded eye, his straight back and outthrust chin, his visage full of promise. Hope burgeoned in their hearts. They willed him to be a true leader, to bring down the corrupt officials, and give his subjects a clear path to peace and prosperity.

The resounding cheers of the assembled masses penetrated the ears of nervous noblemen in their palatial homes. Would the new king cut down their power? Their servants crowded at windows to watch the parade and their children ran outdoors to dance beside the stiff-backed warriors atop rare Arab steeds. Such an ecstatic welcome was beyond the expectations of the aristocrats.

Those who are destined for greatness in life [*the poet wrote, jabbing at his parchment with emotion*], are often tried by fire in childhood. Thus may their mettle be keenly tempered to withstand the blows to come. Such a one was Karikaalan, the first man to bring the southern states together and forge them into a formidable sword against all rivals.

He was born as Peruvalathan to the old, royal house of the Cholas. His mother was a princess of the Velir people who came south many ages ago from Dwarka. The Velirs, who had since carved out many small kingdoms, lived on the fringes of three mighty empires: the Chola in the west, the Chera in the east and the Pandyas in the south.

Peruvalathan of the house of Chola had been crowned when he just five. It was a sinister time for a child to rise to a throne. The mighty Pandyas and Cheras were ever shouldering their way into the kingdom. They were aided by the Velir chieftains, whose loyalties leaned this way and that as they sought to broaden their own small principalities.

These challenges would have been surmountable had the Cholas been united. Instead, the noble families were mired in political baiting and backbiting. They formed factions of Cholas and Velirs, and tore at each other to increase their own might, caring little who got caught in the crosshairs. While they played snake and mongoose, enemies gnawed away at home and at the nation's borders.

Into this turmoil was suddenly placed the young lord, like a lone candle holding back the darkness that seethed with poisonous rodents. Sharp-toothed shadows scrambled high about the tender flame, hissing to snuff it out. When they couldn't kill him, they strove to use him.

After all, the king needed guidance through his minority. Each pack claimed the right to 'guide' him. Uneasy and shifting alliances formed to oversee the child's upbringing. The royal household became a graveyard for ambitions, as one after another, tutors, attendants and courtiers rose and fell. When matters reached a head, the different parties exiled the king altogether.

For the well-being of the kingdom, they suggested, *the king needs an environment more favourable than the capital of Uraiyur. Let him reside in the grand old city of Karuvoor, where his education will not be disturbed by the day-to-day minutiae raised by his courtiers and subjects. There, our lord may peacefully learn all the arts and sciences, and return to rule once he has attained adulthood.*

It became the one deed that led the courtiers to act as one. Naturally, the parties sent spies into the exile's entourage and so consoled themselves that they had quick access to the king… should such a need arise.

The king's uncle Irum-pitar-thalaiyan used the years of his nephew's minority to amass support – at court, in the army, and even among the people. The many clans saw him rising and believed it was only a matter of time before he found a 'legitimate' way to usurp the throne.

The years passed and the people of Chola-nadu grew weary of their crooks of state. First whispers, then outright protests, demanded that the king return and take charge.

The courtiers saw in this a way to check Irum-pitar-thalaiyan. While this tiger stood red-eyed at the gates, what courtier would fear a cub? Together, they proclaimed support for the public's demands and sent a magnificent state elephant to escort Peruvalathan back to the capital.

Even as they feigned allegiance to the Chola, many of the Velirs continued to send battalions to seize the borderlands for themselves. Their private soldiers constantly ravaged the frontier. The Velirs bit at each other's heels too. In this storm of advancing and retreating armies, the people lost their food, trade, fortune, and often, their very lives. The small opposing forces encroached steadily towards the centre.

At this crucial juncture, the royal elephant brought Peruvalathan to the capital. Seeing his uproarious reception, the noblemen were forced to wonder: *Have we just exchanged a worrisome uncle for a worrisome nephew? No, could the nephew be worse? He is the true king after all. And now he is no longer a child, but a youth, well-formed and*

trained in martial arts. This descendant of a warrior race that stretches back to the most ancient songs and chants, will he prove biddable?

In another act of unity, they met and agreed that the king must be kept from state affairs as long as possible. He must not be handed the power they had worked so long to accumulate. He must be guided, persuaded, forcibly if need be, but he must see the good sense in being pliant.

And so the tricky old courtiers greeted him daily, but gave away nothing and only counselled patience. He must be officially crowned, they said, and assured him that auspicious dates were being assessed. Yet, the ceremony was put off again and again. He was drowned in officious records of little importance, inundated with issues that barely mattered, and hemmed in with contradictory advice on the meanest decisions. Peruvalathan realized that the elephant had brought him from one golden cage to another. Here, he was once more confined to a palace and guarded by men who felt no real loyalty to him.

Used to years of such humiliation, the prince did not immediately rebel. Then his uncle Irum-pitar-thalaiyan came to him. With pointed words, he delivered news of the enemy on their borders. With an impassioned plea, he begged the king to find the tiger within him, to rise and save the Cholas or be the last of the lineage. And he laid all his own vast resources at the king's disposal.

Those without who overheard this conversation felt their worst nightmare come true. The most powerful man in the land had banded together with the legitimate ruler, the hope of his people. The noblemen saw their hard-won gains slipping from their greedy grasp.

In a desperate attempt, they waited till Irum-pitar-thalaiyan left, then set fire to the palace and fled. Young Peruvalathan was pacing his rooms, turning over his next move in his mind. Should he trust his courtiers' promises and wait till they crowned him? Surely they must crown him, since a king was needed to defeat the ransacking armies on the border. Or should he believe his powerful uncle and take action immediately?

As he paced, smoke seeped into his room. Peruvalathan began to feel breathless and muddled. He made his way to the door and threw it open, only to draw back in shock as flames leapt towards him. The room beyond was an inferno. Draperies twisted and tore as the fire licked its way upwards, turning the greens and golds to charred threads. Pillars engulfed in a sea of conflagration came crashing down in a haze of rubble.

Blinded by the sudden heat and the blaze, the king turned, stumbled and fell. In that moment, burning debris fell upon him and seared his flesh. He screamed in agony. Using his hands, he began crawling away from the incandescent room.

So this was the measure of his courtiers' sincerity! As he dragged himself inch by agonizing inch, the confrontation with his death did what his uncle's words had failed to do. Peruvalathan found in himself the will to live at all costs. He would live, he swore, and all men would see what he was made of! The tiger long caged and whipped suddenly discovered its mettle. He drew gradually away from the conflagration and made his way to the bay windows at the other end. Much of his lower body was burned, but with the strength of his arms alone, he threw himself over the ledge and began scaling the high wall.

The fire around the palace had, by this time, drawn the attention of multitudes. Irum-pitar-thalaiyan, whose men were stationed about to protect the king, despatched the news to him. The cool-headed veteran immediately amassed his soldiers and charged at the palace walls. There, his men found the king clinging to the high barricades and rescued him. Even as physicians were summoned to treat the wounded king, Peruvalathan barked out orders for the traitors to be seized. His soldiers swept through the court, bringing down known conspirators and killing anyone who resisted. They moved into the city next and, in a fell stroke, the worst of the faction heads were beheaded. Nor did the king spare their families.

Those who could, fled the carnage to their own lands. But like a punishing storm, Peruvalathan swept down upon one principality, then the next, bringing his malcontent cousins and feudatories to heel. Once more the Chola tiger flew fiercely high upon the ruler's flag as his army stalked across the land.

At their wits' end, the remaining Velirs took refuge with the neighbouring Chera emperor.

The Chera ruler, Uthiyan Cheralathan, was no petty adversary. His nation was so prosperous, it fed the vast armies of the north during a long-drawn-out war without damaging its own economy or starving its own people. His port city of Muchiri traded gold, spices, silk and precious stones with far-flung civilizations in Rome, Egypt, Persia and Greece. His armies, particularly the cavalry and elephant units, inspired poets to compose verses of terror that became famous across the subcontinent.

This experienced stalwart mulled over his choices against the newly risen Chola king. Peruvalathan, meanwhile, was on his punitive campaign against the Velirs. On yet another side of his border, the Pandya king, Nanmaran, took the chance presented by his distracted rivals. He invaded north into Chola lands and captured key forts.

The young Peruvalathan now had a conundrum on his hands. To recapture the forts, he would have to take his army well out of its current path. He would also be facing direct opposition from the more experienced Pandya generals.

He chose, therefore, not to protect his own land, but to attack the Pandya king's vassals, targeting strategic Velir principalities that owed allegiance to the Pandyas. Indeed, he razed them to the ground, leaving alive not a blade of grass.

The Pandyas did not take his bait. They would not be enticed into a battle on lands where the enemy had the advantage. But an enraged Nanmaran sent emissaries to the court of Uthiyan Cheralathan. The two allied with eleven Velir kings and set out against Peruvalathan. It was the worst possible outcome for the young king. All the power of the south was now unified against him.

The allied host thundered into Chola lands and pushed them back steadily. They swept all the way up to Uraiyur and threw the king out of his own capital. Still, Peruvalathan did not give in. He racked his brains for a move that would give his rapidly vanishing army a chance in this biased conflict.

He retreated north to a port city. It was his last stand.

Between him and the allied forces lay the city of Venni, famous for many urban distractions. Confident of their victory, the Cheras, Pandyas and Velirs lingered at Venni, enjoying its sumptuous offerings. Their spirits were high from recent triumphs and they saw no reason to rush back to battle. Meanwhile, Peruvalathan raised a fresh army and brought it to the plains outside the city.

Upon seeing the small force camped outside the fort, the massive Chera–Pandya forces laughed in derision. This would be an easy conquest! They opened the gates and stormed out of the fort to meet the Cholas in the open field. After all, what glory was there in defending a fort against such a small force?

The Chola was fully aware of his tricky situation. He had but one strategy that might work: go straight for the centre. A headless serpent is no threat after all. If he could take out the leader, the enemy would lose its will to battle, and melt away. Once decided, he moved swiftly, gambling his all on this one definitive strike.

Peruvalathan put his strongest battalions in the vanguard. He then sat atop a war elephant and led the charge himself. Cheralathan saw him bearing down and grasped the move immediately. The bold assault from so young a general filled him with admiration. Yet, he was confident of meeting it without trouble. He ordered his deadliest elephant units to move against the oncoming Cholas, and himself moved to meet the first wave of the enemy.

In the ensuing battle, the Cholas were desperate for survival. The men were fighting not just for their lives, but for their livelihoods, their homes and families, and a future. Should the Chera and the Pandya win, their very identity could be lost.

Against them was an overconfident enemy, drunk on recent successes, heedless of the adversary, and not particularly motivated by any cause.

In the heat of the battle, the Chola foot soldiers, bearing long, sturdy spears and arranged in deep phalanxes, proved impenetrable to the enemy's elephant battalions. Gradually, they gained the upper hand.

Cheralathan saw the toll it was taking on his army. It would be wise to withdraw and regroup, he determined. With his superior numbers, time was his friend and he could draw out this battle to gain victory. He signalled to his forces to disengage and turned back to lead the retreat. In that fateful moment, the weapon that Peruvalathan sent flying from his elephant pierced the broad Chera back.

As the soldiers watched, the Chera king teetered on his elephant and slumped forwards, unconscious. The shock of the allied army was palpable. The Chola soldiers, jubilant, pressed forward. As Cheralathan's elephant fled the field, the battalions around it panicked. The havoc spread and the men began to flee.

Cheralathan made it back alive to the fort. He was badly wounded, but what he could not bear was that the blade had scored his back. To any warrior, this was a sign of cowardice; a sign that he was injured while fleeing. Cheralathan refused medicine and food, and soon passed away. His bravest companions, unable to part ways, followed him in death.

With the strongest of them gone, the alliance crumbled and each party fled to its kingdom. It was a decisive victory for the young Chola ruler, whom all had underestimated. His triumphant return to his city was marked by joyous celebrations among the people. Not one courtier now dared to raise a word, a look, against the king.

No one could now doubt the might of Peruvalathan. But more importantly, Peruvalathan had found faith in himself. Never would he forget the day his palace was set on fire, nor how the hour brought forth the tiger. For this flaming moment, he would forever more be called Karikaalan Chola – the Chola with the charred leg.

A patter of feet at the door brought the poet out of his writing. His grandson, a lad of five, peeked through the curtain. The poet smiled indulgently and called to him.

'What are you writing?' asked the boy.

'A hero's tale. Would you like to hear it?'

The boy nodded emphatically.

THE DEATH OF CHANAKYA

The queen's palace was chittering like a tree full of bats at sunset. As torches sparked to life against the dying day, rumours flitted between the maids and the changing guards.

It had begun with a ritual.

A cavernous, hallowed hall had been scrubbed clean to welcome the soul of the king's late mother, Durdhara, and the souls of other royal ladies long departed. Great bronze lamps had been oiled and lit. Luxurious robes had been laid out. Auspicious foods had been set out on freshly washed leaves. Then, in a silence redolent with floral perfumes and smoky incense, the court ladies had pulled the doors, creaking, to a close.

The queen, along with the king's other wives, waited for their ancestors' arrival. Her court waited at her side. Among them were maidens and matrons hand-picked for the occasion. Triumphant at having received the coveted invitation, they shone in bright silks and brighter ornaments, their eyes darkly lined, and their hair oiled and festooned with flowers and jewelled pins. There would be a feast later on, where the blessed offerings, robes and ornaments would be bestowed upon them. But first, they must stand in a sea of humid breaths, witnesses to the great royal rite.

As they sweated and fidgeted in hushed anticipation, a wail sounded from the assembled crowd. Eyebrows rose and heads turned in surprise. Again, a long, low-pitched wail like a wounded animal's. The queen's attendants craned their necks this way and that, searching for the source.

Those who were closer to the lament saw a woman fall to her knees. They gasped and moved away, pushing back the crowd. Those beyond, pushed forward in curiosity and a circle formed around the sobbing form. She was rending her hair and groaning, mumbling strange, disjointed words.

Her bun came tumbling down. The flowers fell, pulling at their threads, and an unravelling weave of tresses half hid her face. On a racking breath, she raised her gaze. Those in its path scrambled back to avoid the maddened, searching glare. It flew like an arrow down the long, straight room and caught the queen's eyes. The reddened orbs held the royal ones for a moment, hypnotic, whispering dreadfully.

The queen felt pinned to her throne. She thought she heard that grim murmuring close in her mind. Almost, she felt the woman's breath in her ears. Then, just as suddenly, the eyes rolled back under their lids. The lady fainted. The queen, released from her grip, began to breathe again.

That evening, Bindusara heard the story when he came to his queen's chambers.

'The physicians have seen to the lady, and we have questioned her severely for disrupting the proceedings,' she told him. 'But she remembers nothing.'

'Send her away. She is clearly ill and prone to seizures,' Bindusara replied, dismissive and somewhat displeased that an event of the royal family's should have been so disorganized.

'Now others are saying…' the queen hesitated.

'What?'

'… That… perhaps the soul of our gracious mother… perhaps she is not at rest?'

'Who dares say so?' demanded the king, half astonished, half laughing. 'It has been many summers since Mother passed on. And how many more since you took charge of her remembrance ritual. All this time, she has been at peace. Now some chit of a girl faints and suddenly my royal mother is a restless spirit?!'

'The king is wise and strong,' replied the queen archly. 'If he says it is nonsense, of course it must be.'

She tried to let it go. Then she tried another tack.

'The palace is full of people on the lookout for signs that will favour their purpose. Whispers today are like the breeze that fans small sparks into forest fires. Tomorrow, someone may use this tale to point fingers at us and call us cursed, undeserving.'

'You worry too much,' the king said. 'Do you think a paltry rumour could threaten the Maurya king, the blood of the great Chandragupta, the commander of six hundred thousand infantry, thirty thousand cavalry and nine thousand war elephants, the ruler of an ever-expanding...'

'Really, sire,' the queen broke in. 'Are these the words of one who has been taught by Chanakya! You have seen first-hand how he and your great father ruined vast armies, ruined a whole dynasty, with well-placed rumours! His own laws state that one who spreads evil news about the king must have his tongue rooted out. Were he here, he might question if a more grievous intention lay behind this act. Can we be at peace without knowing the full matter?'

Bindusara pondered this. Perhaps the incident wasn't as simple as it seemed. Was someone pulling strings from the shadows? What could be gained from interrupting a women's ceremony? Perhaps this was just the first move in a larger game. An experienced hunter, Bindusara decided to wait and let his prey approach closer.

The next day, well before the king set out for court, Subandhu turned up at the palace and begged an audience. A matter of some urgency, he claimed.

Bindusara's minister was one of the brightest pandits in government. None other than old Chanakya had marked his talent and recommended him to the post. Bindusara permitted him to enter.

Upon sight of his master, Subandhu fell on all fours and launched into a pother of whining and scraping.

'My gracious king, forgive me for seeking you at this early hour. But indeed, the hour is late for what I have to, nay, for what I *must* say. I fear I have sat too long upon this matter already! I would never dare have delayed so, but indeed, our late king did not say a word. Your teachers, nurses, the loyal old ministers – none has ever said a word. Then how could one as low as I have spoken up? But now, I am ashamed beyond bearing and must confess the whole or resign my conscience and my liege.'

Bindusara's eyes narrowed upon the genuflected figure.

'Arise, Subandhu,' he said sternly. 'And may you speak with care, pandit, seeing that you mention our closest people and dare evoke the late emperor himself.'

Subandhu felt the flame of this warning in a heated rush of blood. Breath misted over his upper lip and he gave his master a moment of respectful silence.

'My king,' he resumed, 'yesterday, I was summoned to interrogate a lady who had caused a scene at the queen's palace.'

'I am aware of this.'

Subandhu bowed. Not daring to meet the king's eyes, he continued, 'O Amitraghata, slayer of enemies, if your servant could answer why the court lady behaved so, would you wish to hear it, even though the answer may bring you pain, and harm one who is closest to you?'

'Since you have said this much, naturally you must speak the whole. Or will my pain make you lose courage?'

'Your pardon, sire, my tongue stumbles and my words are jumbled. But I must be sure, sire. For this is the story of your birth. It is the story of your birth, sire… and more so, the story your noble mother, whose pain and death I have investigated and verified… as you will hear, if you so wish it.'

Gooseflesh erupted down Bindusara's arms like a premonition. Recalling what his wife had said, he spoke coldly, 'My mother died in childbirth. A drop of her blood fell on me, seeing which Chanakya named me Bindusara. Should someone use a fainting girl to gossip about the royal family? Advise me, minister, how should such a courtier be dealt with?'

'Nay, my king, what I have to say is known to all the old servants in the palace. You may command any of them to speak the truth, the whole truth, and this is what you will hear. Indeed, you were born the day your mother died, but she did not die birthing you.'

He hesitated, then continued, 'When heavy with child, none other than Chanakya fed poison to your mother. When she gave up her soul, he slit open her belly and drew you out. Thus it was that he saw her blood fall on you.'

Bindusara shot to his feet, crossed the room and grabbed the minister by his throat. His eyes, bulging and red-veined, bored into Subandhu's wide, terrified gaze.

'You lie!' he bellowed, shaking the slender scholar like a filthy rug. Then he heaved Subandhu aside and turned away, making an effort to regain control.

The minster scurried for the door. He turned, looked at the king's massive back and threw one last piece of advice, 'Ask your attendants, sire, and judge for yourself.'

With that he took to his heels. He did not stop running until he reached his small palanquin. He leapt inside, shouting at his men to move. But only a hoarse sound came from his throat. Impatiently, he rapped on the wood and his men, understanding, picked up and set off.

As they bobbed away from the palace, Subandhu gingerly touched his throat. He tried speaking, but his voice, bruised, was but a gurgling breath. He closed his eyes in resignation. *Nothing ventured, nothing gained,* he thought. If all he lost in this gamble was his voice for a few days, he would count himself very lucky indeed.

At the palace, the king turned his fury upon the room, shredding apart the hangings and turning the furniture into kindling. Then he sent for his nurse.

The moment she confirmed that Durdhara had died consuming food that Chanakya had poisoned, he waved her away. He sent all his attendants out. The room darkened before his eyes as he wrestled with rage and despair. Chanakya, his teacher, his most trusted guide, the man who had created an empire with his father Chandragupta and was like a second father to him. Had the late emperor known of this betrayal? He must have! Why did he allow Chanakya to live?

Restless thoughts twisted into strange questions and unpalatable possibilities.

Outside the chamber, the old nurse worried that all hell was about to break loose. She sent word to Chanakya. When the old minister heard what had happened, he had little trouble piecing together the events that must have preceded it. He ached to his very bones.

I have lived too long, he thought, *to have come to such days. A lifetime proving myself, raising two rulers, building the empire; yet just a few words from a knave have shaken the king's faith in me. I should have followed the old king when he retired to the hermitage. In the end,* thought Chanakya, *he showed himself wiser than me.*

The nurse, who realized that a misunderstanding had occurred, repeatedly sought out Bindusara. But he could not bear to hear more of Chanakya's betrayal and shunned the old woman. Finally, the queen interceded and brought the two together. The matron remonstrated with the king as only an old nurse could do.

'My lord is as impatient now as ever he was when a rash young lad,' she began. But his haggard visage moved her heart.

'Oh, sire,' she said in the motherly tone she had used when he was a boy, 'it is true, as you have heard, that Chanakya poisoned the late queen and cut you out from her belly after she died. But had you not sent me away so precipitously, you might have heard more of that story. Listen well now, how such things came about, and as you do, reflect too that in your haste you very nearly cut down a pillar of your empire!'

Bemused by her words, and curious, the queen too sat down to listen.

'In those days,' the nurse began, 'the old emperor's life was forever in danger. He was mighty. His gains were immeasurable and his enemies uncountable. Despicable creatures! They could not win over him bravely in battle, so they turned to assassins, poisons and underhanded plots to kill him.

'But Chanakya took measures against these attempts. One of his precautions was to mix small doses of toxins into the emperor's food. He increased the dose every day, believing that the king would eventually become immune to poison.

'Alas, Chanakya is wily, and though ever alert, he is also desperately secretive. He kept this matter from the emperor; and, in doing so, is perhaps guilty of what came next. The queen, your mother, was heavy with child. Her time was near and the emperor visited her often. On one such occasion, he affectionately fed her the very food that had been laid out for him.'

The nurse paused. The room became leaden with grief as understanding dawned.

'Chanakya came by chance at the time. He saw the queen in the throes of death and all of us shocked, helpless by her side. As she lay there panting through her final agony, he convinced the king to try and save the baby in her belly. Nothing could be done for her; her pain was unbearable to watch and her lingering endangered the child. Still, the emperor could not end her life with his own hands. So, Brahmin though he was, Chanakya took a knife and slit her throat. Her infected blood ceased pumping poison to her womb. He then sliced open the belly of the lady and drew you out with his own hands.

'Gods be praised that you were alive. But even then, the physicians had little hope of your surviving the shock, the early expulsion from the womb. Again, it was the minister who tirelessly sought a solution. Every day for the next seven days, he had a goat freshly killed, and you were kept safe in its belly. There, you continued to form more fully, gaining health and strength.

'It is for the goats' blood that Chanakya named you Bindusara.'

The nurse ended her story. She looked once more sternly at the king, saying, 'Indeed a man may say Chanakya was responsible for your mother's death. But he would be a scoundrel! See also Chanakya's intentions, sire, and all his actions afterwards. He no less than your father and mother gave you life. And no less has he guided your steps, taught you all you know, been your prime minister, brought talent and riches to your empire, and upheld your reign with the highest honour.'

Bindusara felt the weight of gratitude and guilt bear down on his heart. He flung out of his chambers and set out to Chanakya's mansion. Arriving there, he saw with shock that the place was abandoned. The doors were barred and no one was about. Scouts were immediately despatched to locate the prime minster. Shortly thereafter, the king heard that Chanakya had renounced the world. He had given away all his wealth to the poor, the widowed and the orphaned, and removed himself from the city.

•-•-•-•-•-•-•-•-•-•

More days of worried searching followed. When Bindusara finally found him, Chanakya was seated on a dungheap in the midst of a hot and desolate land. He was visibly thinner, his clothes stained, his lips dry and cracked, his breathing laboured.

Intolerable, thought Bindusara, crushed by remorse. One whom he should have set on a pedestal and worshipped with garlands had been forced into this state by his carelessness. The king approached the old sage and begged him to return to court, seeking forgiveness, insisting that the empire could not do without the experienced minister.

His earnest pleas fell on deaf ears. Chanakya did not relent. In the manner of Jain *munis,* he was determined:

now that his life's mission was over, he would give it up voluntarily. Not a morsel of food would pass his lips, as there was no further need for this earthly body.

Subandhu, whose machinations had thus brought down his superior, was gleeful. But his gaiety turned into apprehension when the king summoned him to the palace. The bruises on his throat were still visible and he was forced to wrap a cloth around it.

In front of the king's rage, he cringed, mumbled apologies and loudly protested his innocence in the matter. No, he had not bribed the girl to create havoc! Nor had he misled his master, but only shared with him a concern for his long-departed mother.

Bindusara cared not.

'Come back with Chanakya,' he commanded, 'or do not come back at all.'

Subandhu seethed, but outwardly, he was all willingness and compliance. He promised to change the stubborn adviser's mind and restore him to court. He gathered up a large and opulent escort for the mission, making a great show of his eagerness to do the right thing. Numerous scholars and members of the court were invited to go along, and a grand chariot prepared to bring back the old minister. Even Radhagupta, Chanakya's beloved grandson, was persuaded to travel in the retinue and add his voice to their cause.

When the preparations were complete, the procession set out to Chanakya's humble seat. It was a desolate place, where the winds – scorching by day, icy by night – whistled through brittle, leafless branches. The procession stopped at a respectful distance and Subandhu alone went forward. As the gathering watched, he kneeled before the platform of dung and hay, humbling himself and coaxing the great Chanakya.

Chanakya neither moved nor visibly responded to this charade. Subandhu returned, shaking his head.

'We may have to set up here awhile and try convincing him again,' he said. 'It is only to be expected that a man so great would not give in so easily. Let us move back a distance – or we may seem troublesome to him – and set up shelter for the night.'

The men led their bullocks back up the wild road and began putting up tents against the fast-cooling evening. Pits were made, piled with wood and charcoal, and fires were lit.

In a few hours, Subandhu announced that he would take some food and a warming pot to the old minister. Perhaps the sight of these renounced necessities would change his mind. So, as the others watched, he took up a vessel of embers in one hand, a meal packed in leaves in the other, and set off to meet Chanakya, who sat like a stone against the cold, windy night.

Subandhu returned empty-handed. When asked, he shook his head again: Chanakya had not responded.

As the night deepened, the travellers broke into companionable groups. The moon had just set when someone commented that the air seemed unusually bright. Suddenly, shouts rang out. Men scrambled to their feet and looked toward the distance. A guard was pointing to the dungheap on which Chanakya sat. It was ablaze, a charred figure clear in the midst of the furnace.

In an uproar, the guards sought water and hides to put the fire out. Radhagupta ran forward howling, but was quickly caught and held back. The flames leapt high, whipped by the wind and dry kindling. The men's efforts proved wretched against it. Chanakya was gone.

When finally the fire gave out, none knew what to say. Subandhu alone set up loud wails. He took charge while others stood stunned, and despatched a messenger to the king. He would stay back – his message concluded somewhat viciously – until Radhagupta had completed the rituals of his grandfather's cremation.

The next morning, however, he sped back to the city and made his way to Chanakya's mansion. *What great gems and treasures lie inside,* he wondered, thinking of the many long years during which Chanakya had been ambassador and prime minister to emperors.

He broke through the bolts, smashed down the doors and scoured the rooms. In a large chamber, he came across a massive chest, chained and secured by what seemed like hundreds of locks! One by one, he shattered the links, his avaricious mind conjuring up precious stones, foreign gold, land deeds, state secrets and ever so much more.

When he finally opened it, there was nothing but a sickly sweet smell inside the box. And a piece of inscribed bark. He wrinkled his nose in distaste and disappointment, picking up the note.

Subandhu, it said, *for what you have done, you are now justly cursed. Whoever smells this perfume and does not renounce the world will face death.*

A rock settled in Subandhu's gut. Had the old fox known all this time? No! How could he? Even Subandhu had not known he would put an ember in the dung-covered seat until the very evening it happened.

Subandhu ran out of the house in a cold sweat. His eyes fell on a scrawny sweeper plying a wretched broom.

'You there!' cried Subandhu. The man looked up and cringed to see that he had been noticed by a rich man. What trouble was this?

'Are you hungry?' asked Subandhu.

Dumbfounded, the sweeper nodded.

'Then, come! Today, you shall eat such foods as only kings and gods find on their table.'

The man shook his head hastily and cowered. 'I am but a poor sweeper, undeserving of such favour,' he mumbled.

'Then make yourself deserving. Be useful to me in a small matter and you may see the food as fair payment.'

'Of what manner would this service be?' asked the sweeper, suspicious.

'Inside this house is a great treasure chest. Only there is no treasure in it! I need someone to look into it and confirm the matter. If you find treasure, that too I will share with you. Now, come!'

The man followed Subandhu inside and came to the great trunk. He opened the lid and scanned inside.

'What do you see?' asked Subandhu.

'Nothing,' said the sweeper.

'What do you smell?' asked Subandhu.

'It is sweet and rotting, but I see nothing from which it could rise. Perhaps something was kept here that left behind such a malodour.'

'Well, if there's nothing, there's nothing. Now come, for your payment, let us eat and enjoy this fine morning!'

With that, he took the sweeper to the wealthiest inn in the city and had them lay out their most sumptuous dishes. The poor sweeper was quite overcome. Was this some test? You never could tell with the nobility. He strained to keep his appetite under control, even as his mouth watered from the meaty aromas.

Then, under Subandhu's encouragement, he dove into the feast and ate like never before. Halfway into the repast, the pleasure on his face was replaced by a shade of purple. Veins stood out around his temples. His eyeballs burst in a shower of gore and his head hit the table. The man was dead.

Subandhu sat stock-still. In his mind, he saw Chanakya playing a game of chess. The dead man looked him in the eye, smiled and said, *checkmate.*

The next day, Subandhu resigned from his post, donated all his wealth and became a monk. A life of severe discipline was still better than no life at all. Radhagupta, who returned from cremating his illustrious grandfather, became Bindusara's new prime minister.

KINGMAKER AND KING

'Mother, it is useless for me to go!' wheedled Ashoka. 'You've seen how my royal father wrinkles his nose at the sight of me.'

Subhadrangi, patting his arm, coaxed, 'The *muni* comes to foretell who the next king will be. The Maurya princes have been commanded to attend, without exception. And your brothers are all making *such preparations* for the event!'

'My *step*brothers you mean. Pah! They are not worth competing with. Father does not see them for the petty creatures they are. I will be king whether or not...'

'Hush!' Subhadrangi clapped a hand on her son's mouth.

Ashoka hushed, but tore away from her and flounced out of the room.

Outside, he ran into Radhagupta, the grandson of the old prime minister, Chanakya.

'Are you here?' Ashoka acknowledged vaguely as the scholar bowed.

'I am here, young lord,' replied Radhagupta, 'to see what preparations are needed. The hour to depart for the golden pavilion is almost upon us.'

'I have heard enough of this. I am not going, I tell you!'

He strode down the hall, flushed and fuming.

Radhagupta rubbed his unshaven chin, calling out, 'And what stops the royal son from following the king's orders?'

Ashoka paused mid-fume.

The Brahmin continued, 'Your mother will give birth to a *chakravarti* – so the prophets foretold and so the king took her into his palace. Now, a renowned *muni* is here to ascertain who among all the princes will be the next ruler. Do you not wish to confirm it for yourself?'

Without turning, Ashoka asked quietly. 'Will a *muni* choose an unfavoured lump like me to be the crown prince?'

Radhagupta's eyes raked over the prince. Ashoka was stunted, pumpkin-faced and covered in blotched, flaking skin. He bowed sadly, conceding the point. The kindest heart would have shuddered to look upon the prince, let alone the inhabitants of the royal residence. Against him, the queens had wielded their wits like talons. His siblings treated him like a ball to be kicked about in their games. Even the attendants dared play upon his esteem with forked tongues. After all, the king had shown no interest in the boy; not since a royal astrologer had pointed out 'inauspicious signs' on Ashoka's body.

Still, for all its ugliness, Radhagupta believed, a gifted and ambitious spirit resided in that body. And he watched over it. And he needled that spirit now.

'My prince, should this sage choose one of your brothers to the high post, would you bow your head to him?'

Ashoka turned and glared, but the scholar went on seemingly unperturbed. 'Why, even your gentle mother did not give up her place, though the other queens bullied her terribly. When she first came to court, a mere scholar's daughter, the other queens raged with jealousy – she was such an unparalleled beauty, you see. By plots and tricks, they sought to suppress her, keep her away from the king and had her trained as a barber!

'Did she give up and run away? Not her! She moved forward step by step in the only way open to her, and by dint of steady hard work, became the king's favoured barber. One day, as she massaged his temples with fragrant oil, the king felt all his worries melt away and fell into a slumber. When he opened his eyes again, he felt light and refreshed.

'Pleased, he offered to grant the barber a wish. And she – what courage it must have taken – asked for a son. Ha! Was the entourage taken aback!

'"Wretch!" cried the outraged chief attendant, "You dare ask the master of the world to father a child with a barber's daughter!"

'Even your father cajoled her, "When a king gives his word, he must stand by it. So, my girl, ask for something else, for this request is inappropriate."

'And the clear-headed lady replied, "I dare not contradict the king. But who may appropriately father my child if not my own husband? Who may appropriately father a future emperor if not the master of the world?"

'You could see the change on the king's face when he recalled his new bride. And he remembered the prophecy attached to her progeny. No doubt it elevated her beauty in his eyes and the two were reunited. When you were born, she named you Ashoka – he who ended his mother's sorrow.

'Though you were named so affectionately, and after such trials, will you now dash all your mother's hopes? And for what? Because those who are jealous and anxious spite you and call you names?'

Ashoka's memory rang with the sneers of times past. *Look at his peeling skin, the worm,* it spat at him. *Oh, be careful, don't step on the warty little toad,* bubbled up a sharp voice. *Did he fall in a pit of night soil?* it cackled. When the furious boy lashed out, the voices cried out in horror, the figures recoiling in case his 'condition' was catching. The abuse grew, as did the boy and his temper. Ugly and violent, he was branded a poison, the vile monster of the Mauryas.

This monster will show you all, he vowed. *Someday, you will be prostrated before me, begging for your lives and you shall see what a monster truly is!*

Radhagupta's words reminded him of his vow. After all, what would the *muni* say? He was curious.

By this time, the two had walked out of Subhadrangi's palace. Ashoka's eyes fell upon an elephant close by the entrance. It stood in the shade, wrapped in silence, the very picture of a haughty beast. Its skin, mottled and wrinkled with age, wrapped over a formidable barrel of a figure. Long tusks curved fiercely below its trunk and scraped the ground. The eyes, though rheumy, held the steadiness of a war veteran. The prince recognized it with a start.

'Why, this grand old battle elephant has long retired from my father's stables! Who brought him here?'

'I did,' replied Radhagupta, 'to be your mount. He is the oldest, noblest steed, though well past his days of glory. Take him. At today's meeting at the pavilion, you will be above all your rivals.'

'They are not my competition,' scorned Ashoka. Nevertheless, pleased and encouraged, he reached out and stroked the elephant. 'I better get going then!' he cried.

The day was a bright hemisphere of blue. Before the royal pavilion of green and gold, it seemed as if a most glorious army had gathered. The many sons of Bindusara filled a vast field from end to end. Each prince was decked to outshine the others in appearance, steed, wealth and retinue. The sun was nearly blinded by their polished chariots, the shimmering silks and gold of their robes, the winking jewels and gleaming armour.

Unfavoured as he was, Ashoka alone had none of these lavish trappings. None, save an old war elephant.

At one end of the pavilion, the king sat in shaded tranquillity with the *muni*. The sage smoothed his hoary beard and looked fixedly upon the princes in turn, ignoring their opulence. He also searched Bindusara's face, noticing how the old king's eye favoured some of his sons and looked displeased upon others.

'You are blessed, sire, with numerous and fine descendants. The line of the great Maurya will prosper no doubt.'

Bindusara waved away the compliment and replied, 'If there is one *chakravarti* among them, it is worth a hundred sons.'

The *sanyasi* looked pityingly at the boys. His eyes fell on a dark shape among all the glitter. Alone, atop a massive grey elephant was a smudge of a youth. He was a curious, strangely revolting figure, yet the *sanyasi* couldn't look away.

King Bindusara followed his gaze and frowned at the sight of Ashoka. The boy's blotched appearance was a constant, taunting reminder of the many red *bindus* speckling his own skin.

'*Munivar*,' he remarked, drawing the sage's attention from his grotesque son, 'see you that young man in the forward row?'

The sage reluctantly drew his eyes to the front and centre. On a finely crafted chariot stood the tall, gay figure of a warrior, arms akimbo, chest and chin thrown up. 'That,' rumbled Bindusara with pride, 'is my eldest, Sumana.'

'A noble mien,' remarked the sage, 'with all the hallmarks.' Though he would not say of what. His glance strayed back to the figure on the elephant.

'Well, now you have seen them all,' said Bindusara. 'Pray tell, who will be king after me?'

The *muni* took in the eager expression of the powerful ruler, considered his eagle-eyed guards, grim-faced generals and wolf-like heirs, and casually patted away the sweat beading his brow. Giving out a name at this juncture seemed deeply unwise. Instead, he rolled his eyes, tilted his head in a knowing way and announced, 'He who sits upon the best mount will be king!'

Disappointed groans erupted from the onlookers. The king agreed with their sentiment. He sternly pressed the *muni* for more.

Upon which, the sage elaborated, 'He who sits upon the most excellent seat, who eats the most wholesome food, who drinks the best drink, who has the superior vessels... he will be king.'

Now this, Bindusara thought, could be controlled. In happy anticipation, he signalled for the feast to begin, giving strict orders for the allotment of seats, vessels and foods to the princes.

Radhagupta overheard the whole story later that day as Ashoka narrated it to his mother.

Subhadrangi asked, 'Are you disappointed?'

The young prince exclaimed, 'Hardly! The royal elephant was my mount. At the feast, the earth itself was my seat. My vessel was made of earth too. Boiled rice with curds were my wholesome food and pure water was my drink. Therefore, I know that I shall be king.'

Such was the eagle-cry of a lofty and irrepressible spirit. In his heart, the prime minister's grandson prayed fervently for the fates to guide the way.

As the months passed, Radhagupta found that many others were beginning to recognize the prince's potential.

The astute politicians and generals of the court could not ignore a man of Ashoka's predatory instincts, or his prowess on the battlefield, and his ever-increasing grasp of strategy and governance. After one hunt, when he killed a lion with nothing more than a wooden stick, even his brothers grew fearful. They begged their father to exile him.

News of Ashoka's gains upset Bindusara. Where others saw an accomplished warrior, he saw an overreaching warmonger.

Should that whelp ever rise to the throne, how many lives will suffer across my empire? Why, my own family will be lost... no doubt of his animosity there! And with the court so closely allied to us, what chaos will ensue. Certainly, Sumana will not survive. Capable, dutiful Sumana... who else can understand and execute my policies half so well?

So ran the king's thoughts.

Soon, he issued an order to Ashoka: *The prince has reached his eighteenth year and is of an age when he must take up duties suitable to his lineage. He will make his way to Ujjain and take up the governance of the principality of Avanti, overseeing it under the laws of the empire.*

Ashoka left the capital. *This will stop him from amassing support in the capital,* thought the king.

However, Ashoka performed his duties firmly. Reports of his tight hold over Avanti were heard at Bindusara's court and gained him allies.

When Takshashila, under the vain rule of an elder stepbrother, rose in revolt, Bindusara sent Ashoka to quell the rebels. *He will fail,* predicted the king, *and his influence in the capital will fade.*

Yet, Ashoka commanded the army well. In his stepbrother's place, he bound the citizens to the

Mauryas once more. Such a feat from one so young had the ministers clamouring for Ashoka to be made crown prince.

When Takshashila revolted a second time, Bindusara sent Sumana to fix the matter. *The ministers will see,* he thought, *my choice is better than theirs.*

Sumana, riding from the palace, met Radhagupta, who was now an experienced minister of the court. In a burst of frivolity, he patted the scholar on his balding pate and passed him by.

Today his hand falls unheeding on my head, thought the Brahmin, humiliated by the overbearing gesture. *Once he is king, it will be his sword that descends on it.*

With renewed vigour, he set about canvassing for Ashoka and leaching away Sumana's support. Meanwhile, reports from Takshashila carried only bad news for Bindusara: his chosen heir was unable to bring the rebellious city to heel. During this time, Bindusara was struck down by a grave illness.

Should I die, thought the king, *the throne must pass to Sumana, not to Ashoka.*

He sent a courier recalling his eldest to the capital and ordered Ashoka to the front, to lead the army in Sumana's place. Many thought the order a validation of Ashoka's abilities and a rebuke to Sumana for falling short on his mission. However, Radhagupta saw through the ruse and waylaid the king's messenger.

While Bindusara lay abed, tossing weakly in his illness, the minister took countermeasures. Quickly, he called an assembly at court. There, Ashoka's powerful allies placed the crown on the prince's head and swore allegiance to him as their future ruler. A triumphant Ashoka made Radhagupta his prime minister.

News of this treason filtered through to the sick chamber. The shock proved too much for the ailing Bindusara and stole his last breath.

Far from the capital, Sumana heard late that the king was dead and a usurper sat on the throne. Wild with grief and rage, he gathered up the army and set out to reclaim his inheritance. He did not doubt that his many brothers were even then fighting to bring the monster down.

Like a many-headed serpent, the royal family rose to corner and strike down Ashoka. But their challenge only pleased the new king. He unleashed years of pent-up resentment. One after another, he caught and slew his stepbrothers, their wives and children, and all the aristocrats, merchants, mercenaries and aides who had backed them.

As the old king had foreseen, fear and turmoil swept through the capital. Soldiers marched through the streets, breaking down doors and dragging away rebels. The wails of terror-stricken victims and doomed accomplices tore through the walls. With every execution, vultures and crows swooped down greedily, attracted by the smell of fresh and rotting flesh.

One alone among all the victims escaped: Sumana's wife, bearing his child in her womb, fled the chaos.

While the king unleashed his rage, the kingmaker plotted his future. Radhagupta kept tabs on the movement of the eldest prince, who approached steadily with the greater part of the empire's army.

The thought worried him little. No, in fact, it rather amused him. His spies had reported how Sumana's troops – suffering from repeated losses at Takshashila – were demoralized. They had little motivation to take up this dynastic fight. After all, what value was there in battling comrades from their own homeland?

Yet, how would a princeling like Sumana, blinded by emotion, see this? Would he spare a thought to raise his men's morale? Would he even have a strategy in place?

Radhagupta resisted chuckling and put his plans into action. He posted lookouts atop each gate to the city. In front of the eastern gates, he had the best craftsmen create a gigantic elephant with a lifelike statue of Ashoka seated on it.

It wasn't long before Sumana approached the city gates and demanded to be let in. Radhagupta stood on the battlements and taunted him!

'If you wish to come in, pay homage first to Ashoka, the mightiest descendant of the great and noble Mauryan emperors. Remove your sword, get to your knees and swear allegiance to the newly crowned king. Then beg his permission to enter his capital. No doubt, the king will be gracious to his brother, even one who so crawls back at the head of a losing army!'

'Bring Ashoka here!' roared Sumana. 'We shall see who bows to whom.'

'That's King Ashoka to you, craven one! Will you meet him in battle? You?'

Radhagupta threw his head back and laughed. His men at the towering gate sniggered at Sumana.

'Even your royal father didn't think you were a match for King Ashoka. Look how he shielded you and kept you apart, lest our mighty leader end you too soon. Go, seek him at the eastern gate if you think you are his equal. Meet him in battle if you can. Perhaps the throne will still be yours, ha!'

In a haze of rage, Sumana spurred his horse around. Radhagupta's jeering guffaws followed him as he hurtled to the eastern entrance. From a distance, he saw his brother seated above a large elephant. Sumana dug his heels into his steed's flanks. Man and horse, frothing at the mouth, charged forward.

As they galloped, the ground suddenly gave way beneath them. Steed and rider tumbled headlong into a deep trench. The gate disappeared from sight while a bed of burning coals rushed up to greet Sumana.

The screams of the dying man and beast rent the air, arresting the soldiers in their tracks. The smell of charred flesh reached their nostrils, confirming the loss of their leader. They threw down their weapons and surrendered. Radhagupta's men opened the gates and arrested the captains.

It took four bloody years after the death of Bindusara for Ashoka to finally suppress all his opponents. Only then was he officially crowned with all the rites and rituals. His childhood enemies now submitted, but his inner demons, grown monstrous since childhood, were very much his masters. And where monsters reign, all is hell.

CHANDASHOKA BREAKS OUT OF HELL

Radhagupta's greying temples dampened with sweat as he paced back and forth, furrowing the earth outside the execution grounds. His back, hunched like a tense bow, shot up straight when a cohort of royal attendants clattered behind him shouting, 'Clear the way! Clear the way for the king!'

The prime minister turned and squinted into the distance. A group of queens was approaching, dressed lavishly, coldly silent. Leading them was the very short – *the very royal,* Radhagupta corrected himself – figure of Ashoka, in robes of white and gold. They drew closer and Radhagupta bowed before his master's fierce gaze. When he looked up again, he noticed the thinly veiled revulsion on the faces of the royal wives.

Radhagupta held back a frustrated sigh. *Sour-faced, stubborn fools!* he cursed. *How blindly they disdain him even now. There will be another bloodbath if they don't watch out – already, he is smiling with his teeth.*

'You appear at the right time, Radhagupta,' said Ashoka, his eyes red-veined and maliciously gleaming, 'and in the right place.'

'It is one of my many talents,' smiled the minister, ignoring the apprehension turning his stomach upside down. 'How may I serve you, lord?'

'I see you're coming from our most pleasant theatre,' replied Ashoka, his eyes upon the distant scaffold with its ominous hanging figures. 'Was today's entertainment to your liking?'

'You write a most fearsome play, sire,' acknowledged Radhagupta. 'Perhaps it should not be narrated here, in the presence of gently bred ladies.'

The king turned and gazed at the icy beauties. 'Not at all,' he said, sneering. 'My wives are descended from terrifying generals and tyrannical ministers. Would they shrink from a little gallows drama? My dears, shall we narrate for you what is being staged over there? Ho, I take your silence as assent. Well, you shall hear and say – have I judged your fibre correctly?'

'The groves and gardens of a certain city,' he began, 'were filled with the most garish flowers and the ripest, stickiest fruit. They proved a great distraction in the king's eye, which found beauty in only thorny trees. He ordered, therefore, for all trees to be cut down save the bare ones that pleased him.

'"What is Your Majesty planning?" objected his courtiers. "Is it not more beneficial to cut down the thorny trees and preserve the ones that bear flower and fruit?"

'Ha! The king, being magnanimous, gave them many chances to obey his word. Thrice, he ordered all but the thorny trees to be cut. And thrice, oh, some five hundred courtiers turned a deaf ear.'

Ashoka paused as an attendant came hurrying forward from the gallows. 'What do you think of the plot so far?' he asked the audience as the attendant kneeled and saluted the two men. No one replied as all eyes watched the attendant offer up a sheaf to the minister.

'This record confirms the five hundred men executed this day,' he said.

'Read it out, Radhagupta,' the king commanded.

The minister broke the seal and began reciting the names and ranks of the criminals. He addressed the king and dared not look beyond. At first, there were disbelieving gasps from the women. These soon turned to wails and swooning cries as familiar names fell upon their ears – names of fathers and grandfathers, brothers and uncles.

When all the royal ladies and their maids had fallen to their knees in tears, many trembling in a faint, others screaming for mercy, Ashoka stopped his minister.

He looked at the quaking, defeated bodies at his feet, pleased. 'Well, now you know how the play ends. Ah, never mind, my dears, your husband is still around, even if you have lost your fathers and brothers. You would not want such shallow and disloyal men to trouble our kingdom, would you?

'And don't you cry for the pretty trees either. The magnificent *ashoka* still stands in our garden. Rejoice, my queens. Let its flaming beauty comfort and fill your hearts. Come, Radhagupta, we have work to do.'

The king strode back down the path, away from the execution grounds. Radhagupta cast a pitying eye at the scene behind and followed. The women gathered themselves and flew towards the execution platform, where the bodies of their loved ones had been taken down and stretched out.

When Ashoka returned to his palace that evening, he took his cowed wives out to the garden. In that bleak expanse, dotted by hacked stumps, only his namesake tree stood pristine.

'This dark, rough trunk, so sturdy and widely branched; it is like me,' he murmured. 'And each branch, lost in a profusion of jade leaves and tight blossoms like flaming snowflakes; why, this is like you, my dears. Behold how beautiful is the *ashoka*!'

The women agreed with faltering enthusiasm. After he fell asleep, they pulled away to the cool verandah. Out of his hearing, they vented their grief in a cacophony of sobs, complaints and curses. Their companions and maids gathered about, clucking in sympathy.

'For such a whim has he cut down the greatest, the noblest houses to their roots. Oh fathers, brothers, who will stand up for us now? How will we bear your loss?'

The attendants hissed. 'Better to blossom in a field of dry grass – and be trampled to dust! – than spend a minute blooming on that scabrous *ashoka*. Oh, the poor ladies.'

'Must we bear it alone?' demanded a resolute queen. 'Why should we suffer inexpressible agonies while he sleeps free in his conscience! Do we allow such a crime to pass without returning a single strike? For our families… without a single act of retribution?'

And so the queens set to work, thinking no further than the immediate need to cause Ashoka pain, and assuage their own.

Well before dawn, Ashoka rose, bathed, dressed and then summoned his secretary. When the morning had lightened his labour a little, he rose and strolled towards the palace gardens. The bare hedges, the axed stumps, the bleached grass – he took them in by turn, smiling as one who holds power over his world. Then his eyes fell on the scarred *ashoka*.

Someone had plucked out all its proud flowers and trampled them to the ground. The king shook with anger. There would be no rest while such traitors remained close by. In a haze of red, he ordered his wives and their maids be seized and questioned. Five hundred in all – queens and servants – confessed under torture.

The wilful harm done to the mighty *ashoka* was recorded, and in punishment, all five hundred guilty women were burned alive. News of the king executing his family spread outside the palace. Tales of his pitiless acts spread and grew in horror with each telling, and a new nickname arose: Chandashoka, the monstrous.

In his ministerial chambers, Radhagupta considered the numbers losing their lives to the king's pride… and the numbers that were no doubt in line next, when Ashoka's ire rose again. As if in answer to his musings, a sentry announced that a delegation of ministers requested audience. Radhagupta rose and greeted the men, his fellow survivors under a mercurial ruler.

'Chancellor,' the tenacious ones said to him, 'descendant of the great Chanakya', they begged, 'surely you know why we are here today.'

Radhagupta wordlessly invited them to take a seat.

After some hemming and hawing, they said, 'Since ancient times, it has been the right and responsibility of kings to prescribe just punishment. Brahma himself created the royal staff of force to protect the world and allow men to perform their duties. But *danda* is a terrifying beast with many arms, legs, tusks and eyes. It is meant to strike fear in the hearts of those with ill intentions. But that cannot be the only face of the king. He must also be the benevolent spring sun that nourishes growth.'

'Good sirs, you will find no argument with me,' replied Radhagupta. 'One who reviles the king or betrays his counsel must have his tongue rooted out. One who attacks the king's palace must have his hands and head set of fire. These are just punishments carried out by our lord. Or do you question this?'

The ministers hastened to reassure him.

'We do not question the punishments nor the king's rights to punish traitors. But the king's actions must be acts of state, not personal. He must be seen to protect his people. Have you not heard, though, what the people have been calling their lord?'

Radhagupta rubbed the bridge of his nose. 'I understand you, gentlemen. But we can hardly say as much before the throne. Unless you wish to go the way of the last one thousand… What do you propose?'

The ministers eagerly said, 'In a village in the foothills, there is a weaver's son called Girika. Though a young lad, he has struck fear in the hearts of all living creatures there. He bullies the weak and beats up his fellows for sheer pleasure. And when he is bored, he traps and tortures small animals. Nor does he respect or mind his parents. Such a vile temperament may be turned in favour of the state. Make him the executioner, O Radhagupta, and the king may step away from the tortures and executions. And who is to say, but free from such acts, he may eventually cease pursuing them in thought as well.'

Radhagupta recalled the unquenchable rage that ever smouldered like glowing embers in his liege's coal-black eyes. On the battlefield, it was a blessing. But in times of peace, such egregious acts could unsettle the kingdom.

The audience took place in a gazebo newly erected for the king to admire his stark gardens. Its temporary awning hung heavy above the royal head, providing shade but little other relief. Radhagupta shared the structure's meagre solace, while Girika stood without, eyes screwed up against the glare of the scorching sun. He was a great gorilla of a man, and it was easy to believe him a bully.

'Are you willing to take up the post of state executioner, boy?' asked Ashoka.

Girika grinned impudently and replied, 'Assuredly, sire! Why, I could execute all of Jambudveepa with relish and craft for each a different death!'

Ashoka was delighted. 'And if you had to obtain confessions before execution?'

'I defy any criminal to stay silent after going through a few rounds with me, hah! My methods will obtain any confession my lord desires.'

'What methods and deaths would you devise?' Ashoka asked.

'On my way here,' Girika replied, 'I overheard some Buddhists preaching and it came to me that their ways are indeed the best. Sire, have you heard them describe the structured tortures of Hell? The wardens of Naraka, they said, bind evildoers with a fivefold punishment. They drive a red-hot stake of iron through one palm, one more through the other palm, a third and a fourth through the feet. Finally, they drive a red-hot iron stake through the centre of the chest. There lies the sinner, racked by burning, piercing pain, yet unable to die as long as his evil karma is not consumed.'

Girika trembled in ecstasy as he spoke, his imagination blossoming darkly under his own words.

'The wardens stretch out the man on the ground and slice him with axes,' he continued. 'Then they string him up feet first and shave slices off vertically with adzes. He is harnessed to a chariot and driven over and over across a

glowing plain of coals that erupts in flames. At the base of a burning mountain, he is let loose and prodded into climbing up and down its blazing slopes. Then they plunge him headfirst into a giant copper cauldron bubbling with molten metal. As he boils in the cauldron, the foam brings him now up, now down, and now all round and round. Yet, he does not die as long as his bad karma is not consumed.'

As Girika's words twisted and turned within a maze of cruelties, the king grew more and more enamoured. Eventually, a plan was made between them to mimic the many horrors of this Hell.

The king would build a special place to send his enemies to be tortured. Yet, it would be camouflaged as a pleasure garden, beautiful and unfenced. Girika was attentive to every detail from its relaxing bathhouses and flowered walkways to the fountains and statues. In all possible ways, it looked like paradise on earth. Only those who were caught in its trap would know that Girika was equally attentive to the hell within.

When the garden was ready, Girika rubbed his hands gleefully and submitted to Chandashoka, 'Sire, grant me this boon: that whoever enters this place shall not leave it alive.'

The king granted his wish and commanded, 'Go forth and begin your task!'

Girika carried out such heinous acts in the garden that he was given a nickname to match his master's. He was called Chandgirika. The tales of his doings spread far and wide, and did much to raise Ashoka's reputation as a fierce ruler.

Then came the war with Kalinga. The nation was smaller than the Mauryan empire, but a strong nation for all that. In the eighth year of his reign, the descendant of Chandragupta Maurya set out to conquer the peaceful and prosperous state that had successfully repulsed his grandfather's mighty armies. Ashoka led his troops against a final battle with the smaller but equally valiant Kalinga army.

When it was over, he stood victorious on the battlefield and looked about at hundreds of thousands of bodies. Thieves slunk between the corpses, stealing weapons, armour, coins and anything they could carry away. Great vultures swooped in to ravage the ripening carcasses, pecking out the livers and playing ball with the eyes. Around them scavenged monstrous hyenas, ripping bones out of sockets, quarrelling and cackling. Worms infested the blood-drenched grounds and the incessant buzz of meat flies rose above all.

The horror of his actions finally seeped into Ashoka's consciousness. It was as if the red rage that had blinded him seeped away and into the ground. As his vision cleared, the weight of the wretchedness he had inflicted bore down upon him. His shoulders bowed and his knees buckled under the unbearable guilt.

When he returned to the capital, he sought out the evil gardens, intent on tearing them down. He found Girika there – near-mad from years of torture and murder. The scarred creature hovered in the shadows by the entrance.

Unaware of Ashoka's intention, but recognizing his master, Girika warned him. 'My lord, you granted me a boon,' he said, 'that none would leave this place alive.'

Ashoka was taken aback at the effrontery and demanded, 'What? You want to execute me?'

'Undoubtedly,' replied his eager enforcer.

Ashoka stood for a moment in thought. Then asked, 'Which one of us entered this place first, Girika?'

Chandgirika admitted, 'I did, sire.'

'Then you must be the first to die.'

In consternation, Girika saw that it must be so. Yet, he fought when Ashoka's men arrested him. He fought when they reached the execution grounds, where the warden of hell was burnt alive. The hell itself was demolished by Ashoka and all its prisoners reprieved.

It is not to be supposed that this single act freed Ashoka of all the guilt that had piled up from his many violent acts. It was but the first step on a long path of penance. But that step had at least led him out of hell.

GUNADHYA AND THE BOOK OF BLOOD

It happened on a day that Satavahana took his many wives and followers on a pleasure trip to the banks of the Godavari.

There, the happy party stumbled across a garden that invited cries of joy and wonder. Trees with fat trunks spread their branches wide, offering a cornucopia of ripening fruit. Curtains of pendulous flowers shivered in the scented breeze. A festival of birds chattered and flitted through the aromatic underbrush, gathering nectar into their portly bellies. Here and there, the river water snaked into fountains and streams that sparkled in the sun. Long-beaked storks stood single-legged in the pools, darting occasionally at stout fish that swam by.

As they sauntered down the soft grassy paths, the women grew ever more mischievous and playful. They discovered a shallow, shaded lake and waded into it, gasping as the cool waters hit their legs and bellies. The king dove in with a big splash, setting them all laughing and squealing.

One of the queens cried out, '*Modakaistaadaya*!'

Hearing her, Satavahana cried out to an attendant on the shore, 'Ho there! Bring us some *modaks*.'

The man ran and fetched a trayful of the sweet dumplings to the lakeside and knelt to offer them to the queen.

The lady laughed at this.

'Oh, how could you think I wanted to eat sweets while swimming!' she teased Satavahana. 'My husband, I clearly said *maa – udakaih – taadaya* (don't splash the water about). Is the king of the land not familiar with Sanskrit?' The others around her giggled.

The king flushed. His jaw clenched and his face grew stern.

Dismay spread through all as they watched the offence burrow into their lord's eyes. In the awkward silence, Satavahana stomped out of the lake. His servants scurried after to help him change.

By the time he came back in fresh robes, the group had fashioned a forced, if fragile, cheer. But the king sat among them morose, waving away plates of food and drink, and shrugging off remarks addressed to him.

Every smile he saw made him glower in suspicion. *Are they smirking at me behind that facade?*

Every laugh that floated to his ears earned a sharp glare. *How dare they,* he seethed. *How. Dare. They!*

When they returned to the palace, he barricaded himself in his chambers and refused to let in either minister or servant. When matters did not improve the next day and the day after, one wise attendant sought out the king's favoured advisers, Gunadhya and Sarvavarma.

'The daughter of Vishnushakti,' he told the two men, 'is no real scholar. Who is she to question the king's... ahem... Well, even her father has only a shallow learning. And haven't we all suffered, at one time or another, from his pompous wit!' he grumbled, rolling his eyes. 'Little wonder such a queen would utter thoughtless words. Only, they have misled our leader to doubt himself.'

'I have seen shadows of this before,' Sarvavarma said, 'The king has always questioned the depth of his learning. He must think his weakness has now been revealed to all.'

'And no doubt,' added Gunadhya, 'the courtiers' well-meaning efforts to lighten the mood afterwards only made it worse. He must have thought they were taunting him for being unaccomplished.'

The following day, the servant persuaded the king to speak to the two grammarians.

'You never could turn away men of high knowledge, sire,' he said cleverly, and Satavahana felt obliged to give in. He met with the scholars.

When the three of them were seated, Gunadhya began impatiently, 'Noble lord, when the potter is distracted, his clay becomes unruly. When the teacher is distracted, his students become capricious. When the ruler is distracted from his duties, all his realm becomes subject to the vagaries of chance and mischief. Your servants and ministers daily worry for the well-being of king and state. For what tremendous reasons have you shut yourself away from us all?'

This overbearing speech went into one ear and slid out the other. King Satavahana remained brooding, his gaze upon the floor, his grip tight upon a cushioned armrest.

Sarvavarma then spoke up more gently.

'O king! Not long ago, you asked me, "Will I ever be a true scholar?"'

Satavahana's gaze shot up. Pleased to get his attention, Sarvavarma continued.

'That same evening, I chanted a mantra for prophetic dreams before going to sleep. In the dream that followed, I saw a radiant boy who stood in the skies and made a white lotus blossom. He threw the flower down from high above. From where it fell, there arose a wise woman all robed in white. I saw her enter the king's mouth. At this, I awoke.

'Having thought it over, sire, I am certain that the divine lady now resides on your tongue. And that she is none other than Devi Saraswati. My king, what think you of this dream?'

Satavahana's golden gaze held steady on the narrator. He turned over the words in his mind. Then, he took a deep breath and said, 'Learning is true wealth. Without it, a king is no better than a rich fool. If the Devi has indeed blessed me, then I must take pains to gather the wealth she bestows.'

Sarvavarma and Gunadhya smiled, their relief evident.

'Good scholars,' continued the king, 'we will not speak of my ignorance.'

The two men loudly differed from this supposition, but Satavahana stopped them with a wave of his hand.

'We will *not* speak of it,' he reiterated firmly. 'Instead, tell me: were I to make a real effort – were I to persevere without break – how long think you before I become truly erudite? By the highest standards.'

High-minded Gunadhya replied, 'O king! Grammar is the doorway to all other paths of knowledge. It takes twelve years to master it. But if you persist, I will help you become proficient in just six years!'

In a flash, Sarvavarma declared, 'My king, I will help you become a master in just six months!'

Gunadhya stood up, his eyes flashing.

'Impossible!' he harrumphed. 'Is this a game?'

'Why do you say so!' retorted Sarvavarma. 'Do you doubt my ability? What I have promised, I shall achieve. Do not take me so lightly!'

'Ha! If you can perform such a feat in six months... why, it is out of the question!' Gunadhya scoffed.

Sarvavarma sprang up and vowed, 'If I do not keep my word, I shall carry your shoes on my head for twelve years! And you? What will you do if – no, *when* – *when* I succeed, what will you do?'

Gunadhya's eyes narrowed. 'It is impossible, I say. But if you do manage it, I shall abandon speaking the languages of mankind – Sanskrit, Prakrit and all other human languages.'

The grievous words rang out and echoed through the shocked chamber. As if splashed by cold water, the two scholars came to their senses and realized they had gone too far. But the words had been spoken, and before the king at that! They could not go back on their oaths without losing credibility. So, they reaffirmed their promises to Satavahana. Cheered by their assurance, the king sent them back and returned to his duties.

Back home, Sarvavarma became deeply troubled.

What possessed me? he wondered. *This task is impossible, just as Gunadhya says.* He cursed the passing kick of rivalry that had pushed him into this quagmire of a situation. *A scholar?* he disparaged. *No! What a thoughtless oaf I am!*

With a fervent prayer to his gods, he took up his quill and began to chart out a six-month plan to turn the king into a scholar.

♦·♦·♦·♦·♦·♦·♦

When the half year was over, King Satavahana stood up to be tested and proved himself an erudite man. All were surprised, none more so than Sarvavarma. But this was drowned in the tide of praise that engulfed the royal figure. The king's guru could not have been more rapturous! In *guru-dakshina,* Satavahana gave him the province of Marukaccha on the banks of the River Narmada.

The king even raised the daughter of Vishnushakti, whose playful words had started his transformation, to the position of high queen.

Gunadhya, however, had lost his bet. And oh, to what depths the mighty one now fell. One of the most respected intellects of the time was rendered mute. His vow forbade him to speak or write in any human language.

All his great learning became useless. What could he do, if he could not teach, advise or publish? In an instant, his bright future vanished. He embraced foul defeat in his heart and left the city. Only two loyal disciples, Gunadeva and Nandideva, followed to serve him.

Still, where could Gunadhya go? What could he do?

When he was still a boy, Gunadhya had lost all his family except for his grandfather. In those tough times, fate and effort had taken him to schools in southern India. It was there that he became an expert in languages and gained renown as a scholar. Now, as if by instinct, his steps led him southwards once more.

On this long walk, he entered the Vindhya forests. As he stumbled deeper and deeper under the dark canopy, it seemed as if the demons of hopelessness from within him had come out to keep him company.

From time to time, he was certain he saw these monsters, red-eyed and sharp-fanged. Yet was the darkness so heavy, both within and without, that he walked on without much care. It wasn't until one of his disciples hissed '*Pishacha!*' that he became aware of the very real danger.

The three men came to a halt. Around them, *pishacha*s winked in and out of sight. Recalling tales of these fierce, flesh-eating creatures, Gunadhya stared into the gloom and thought, *Is this my end?*

Yet, for all their bloodthirsty reputation, the *pishacha*s left him alone. Over the following weeks, they were always around, but they did not bar his way nor trouble him.

In the great stillness of the forest and through his own enforced silence, words had begun to leave Gunadhya.

His mind became still and clear. Unburdened by past knowledge, his powers of listening grew and his curiosity became as fresh as a child's.

With surprise, he began to notice that the *pishacha*s spoke with each other. As his senses grew sharper, he caught on to their words, matched them with gestures and actions, and began to understand the forest dwellers.

Each day, Gunadhya gathered new words as avariciously as if they were rare gems. And it was not just their words he gained, but a whole new way of thinking, of looking at the world. The extraordinary ideas and views of these beings, so cut off from civilization, broadened his horizons.

How much more there is to life than humankind, he thought. The joy this new language brought was like monsoon to his fertile mind. Gunadhya felt great compositions thundering through his veins. He pierced his arm. As the living blood spilled out, he used it as ink and began to write.

For seven inspired years, he crafted stories in the language of the *pishacha*s. When he was done, the work was seven hundred thousand verses long! And there was nothing to compare it to.

Gunadeva and Nandideva saw that their master had exhausted himself in completing a remarkable work. They heard his miraculous compositions and urged him to take the book out into the world.

Gunadeva went one step further.

'Remember, wise one, how the king values literature,' he said.

'Yes,' nodded Nandideva, 'and when you first arrived at his capital, recall how the royal one heard of your presence and rushed to greet you. The grand retinue behind him too, they were all so curious about the new genius in their midst. You had barely spoken an introduction when the king begged you to stay and become a part of his court.

'Surely he will see that this work is without peer, teacher, and that it must be cherished and passed on to other scholars.'

Thus, after much coaxing, hope revived in Gunadhya and he travelled back to the city with his new work. He waited on the outskirts and sent his disciples with the written sheaves to court.

The king, however, was deeply offended.

'Seven hundred thousand verses?' he scoffed, 'In the gibberish of those inhuman *pishachas*? Can their unintelligible screeching be called language? Can this work be called literature? And he dares submit it to us in this form: scratched out in dirty dried blood! Fie! Throw this abomination out!'

Gunadhya's heart broke when a messenger threw his precious sheaves at his feet and repeated the king's words to him.

As he wandered the woods on the outskirts, he came to the conclusion that, indeed, his work was not meant for the human world. He would therefore sacrifice it to the gods.

He built a great fire pit, consecrated it with chants and began his offering. Page by page, he narrated the stories to anyone who would listen, reading every page and committing it to the blazing fire. His sonorous voice rose on the wind and rang through the woods. Soon, the animals and birds in the forest, enchanted by his narrative refrain, drew closer.

While he was thus busy burning his masterpiece, the king had fallen ill. Satavahana lost the will to address the kingdom's matters, and spent his days listless and dissatisfied. The doctors who came to see him advised him to eat wild meat and regain his energy.

Hunters were despatched to bring the meat. But search as they did, they could not find any deer, bison, boar or prey of any sort. That is, until they heard the resounding chants. Following it to the source, they saw all beasts great and small gathered before the scholar.

News of this peculiar occurrence roused the king from his slumberous state. He set off with his equally curious court to the woods.

There they saw Gunadhya, his hair matted, his robes threadbare, seated amid a host of wild animals. The creatures were mesmerized by the moving baritone and the periodic blaze of flames as Gunadhya sobbed and burnt another page. The scene lifted the veil from Satavahana's mind.

He immediately prostrated before the scholar and begged him to stop burning the pages.

Leading Gunadhya away from the fire pit, he confessed, 'Having received acclaim for my Sanskrit, I have grown conceited. And from that conceit, I have perhaps grown fearful, for your groundbreaking work has put me back at square one – as a man of no great learning.

'What folly it has been to ask you to sacrifice human language. And what a strange blessing. For, noble Gunadhya, you have created, from scratch, a whole new way of thought. Forgive my vanity and let me hear more of it.'

Gunadhya replied, 'O king, only one of the seven stories is remaining. I have burnt six stories consisting of six hundred thousand verses already. Take this *Brihatkatha*, the last hundred thousand verses; my disciples will explain them to you!'

So saying, Gunadhya handed the opus to the king, renounced the world and was thus truly liberated from his curse.

BEAUTY AND THE BEAST OF BENGAL

The king of Vanga married a princess of Kalinga. In time, a daughter was born to them and they named her Suppadevi. On her naming ceremony, the king invited renowned soothsayers to look into her future and predict how her life might turn out.

The old men of Vanga inspected the child, muttered formless words, peered into the smoke of holy fires and prophesied: *The princess will one day be consort to the king of beasts.*

The foretelling caused some alarm in the palace. To ensure that such an event would never come to pass, the princess was all but imprisoned in the palace. She was discouraged from exploring her surroundings, and strictly commanded to avoid all company that wasn't sanctioned and scheduled.

No beast, the royal parents determined, would ever catch a glimpse – not a whiff! – of their gentle daughter. She was taught to hide herself, to melt into the background, to walk softly, to speak in whispers and to veil her face.

Some, who pitied her, taught her how to defend herself, should the prophecy ever come true. And this she liked best. For she did not, as her well-wishers hoped, submit quietly to a restrictive upbringing. Suppadevi brimmed with life. Her free, cheerful ways and precocious mind constantly led to mischief and inevitable punishments. The king and queen did not entirely approve of so spirited a daughter – so outspoken and unrefined, they rued, commiserating with each other – and imposed more restrictions upon her each day.

With each passing year, the yoke became heavier. When it became much too much to bear, Suppadevi put her training to good use and stole away from the palace. She planned her escape. She hid herself cleverly, melting into the background and tiptoeing ever so softly that no one saw her leave.

The world was now at her feet and its vastness left her both breathless and a little fearful. Dressed in a servant's clothes, she paid a caravan of merchants for safe passage away, out of the capital. They accepted her money and gave her a place on a cart.

Soon the cavalcade was on its way, moving steadily north past towns, farms and open countryside. In the province of Lada, the procession paused by a shallow stream. The commuters got out to stretch their legs and chat with each other while the animals and drivers flocked to the cool water to quench their thirst.

Suppadevi looked about her in wonder. On one side stretched a winding ribbon of steep, broken hills, some bare and veined like a bald head and others lost in greenery so dense, she could easily imagine them crawling with leopards, bears and dholes. She strained her ears and imagined the trumpeting of an elephant, the hacking cough of a panther from beneath that verdant canopy.

Never had Suppadevi felt such an ecstasy of freedom.

The awe was short-lived as, suddenly, the rear of the procession erupted in shouts and screams. The caravan masters up front immediately called guards to action. As people came fleeing forward, the mercenaries who had been hired to protect the merchants and their goods gathered and bore down in the opposite direction.

Suppadevi gawped, her calves tensed to flee, yet rooted to the spot by her curiosity. A band of outlaws dressed in coarse skins and furs were charging out of the green cover. They forded the stream and upturned the rearmost carts, quickly forming a shield. There, they clashed with the guards. While some of the brigands fought, their fellows made steady raids on the caravans, hauling away the loot into the jungle.

The marauders were led by a mammoth of a man. Covered in lion skin, with the beast's skull for a helmet, he shook the confidence of the men opposing him. Against his deafening roars and unrelenting power, the guards were forced to fall back. More loot fell to the bandits.

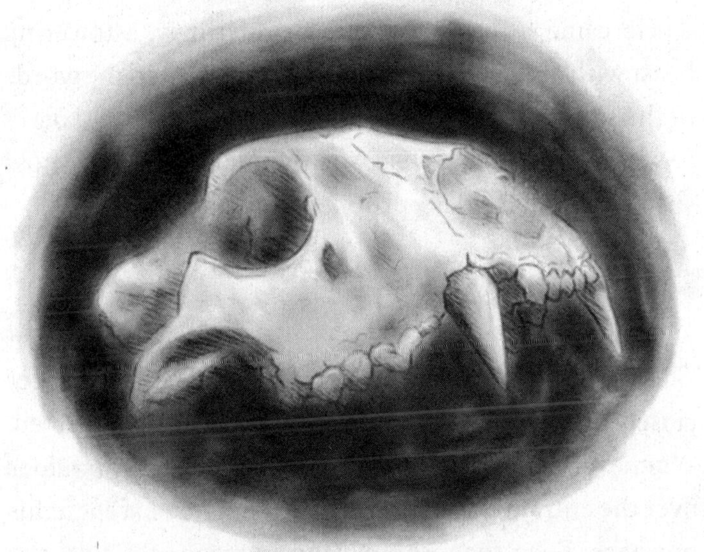

In the rising dust and mayhem, Suppadevi was the one point of utter stillness. The lion, surveying the battlefield, spotted her. His eyes narrowed.

With the fluid power of a predator, he leapt over cart and body until he landed before her. Gathering her up as if she were no more than another sack to be hauled away, he called retreat. Instantly, his men disengaged with the merchants' army and sprang back into the depths of the veiled slopes.

The caravan, the stream and the guards – who did not give chase – vanished before Suppadevi's eyes as the bandits raced back to their forest home. Where they parted ways with the band she did not see, but soon she found herself alone in a cave with the lion.

He came to her hesitantly, wonderingly, a towering beast with glittering eyes. But she remembered the words of the soothsayers. She was not afraid. *So this is the king of beasts written in my destiny,* she thought. And this is how she believed the elders' prophecy had come true.

The lion loved his new consort and guarded her closely. Once more, Suppadevi found herself restricted. Whenever he left the cave, he would roll a large boulder over the entrance. He never allowed her out, except in his presence. Even then, she met no humans, not even the other outlaws in the forest.

To this strange couple was born a pair of twins: a girl and a boy. As they were the children of a *simha* (lion), the princess named her daughter Simhasivali, and her son

Simhabahu (one who had the powerful arms of a lion). The lion was greatly enamoured of his family, cherished them deeply and, in his savage way, kept them safe – trapped in the cave.

Thus, his love did not inspire an equal return. Like Suppadevi, her growing children yearned to roam freely. To all three of them, the lion was little more than a jailer who fed them periodically and kept them tied to a gloomy prison. As the years passed, the children noticed great differences between their mother and father.

Mother taught them to read and write. She taught them to dance, paint, debate, fight, But best of all, she told them stories of many glorious things beyond their imagination. She spoke of palaces, of strange people and of mysterious, never-before-seen objects. Father did none of these things.

When he was sixteen, Simhabahu proved himself truly the princess's child. 'You and father are so different, dear mother. Why do we not run away from here and go back to world from which you came?'

Suppadevi agreed with him, but sighed, 'If only your father were not so careful about placing a barrier in our path.'

In anguish, Simhabahu ran to the entrance and pushed at the rock. Rage over their predicament overtook his senses. The boy with the arms of a lion set his shoulder to the boulder and heaved it with all his maddened strength. The granite groaned, then gave way and went crashing down the forest.

After nearly two decades, Suppadevi was free once more. She and her children rushed out in the wake of the boulder and soon found their way to a rough-hewn road. By feeding on wayside herbs, small animals and fish, they laboriously made their way out of the forest and chanced upon a village.

Here, they found a small army had made camp. The soldiers were making use of peacetime to strengthen the border areas. Their commander was seated under a banyan tree, overseeing the construction, when he spotted the dust-covered woman and her two young companions stumble out of the forest.

Pitying the trio for the evident hardships they had faced, he bade his men give them a place to rest and wash, and provide them fresh clothes and food. When the three came later to thank him, the commander was taken aback upon seeing Suppadevi. The way she carried herself, her refined speech, even her manner of eating, convinced the commander that this was the daughter of a noble family.

Further conversation led to a full narration of Suppadevi's life. The enthralled commander carried her and her children back with him to the capital of Vanga. The princess however made him swear not to reveal her whereabouts to her royal parents. The commander agreed and offered his own home as shelter. Suppadevi acquiesced and the two were immediately wedded.

Meanwhile, the lion, upon returning to his cave, roared with grief and rage to find his family gone. Seeking his wife and children, he wandered across the province until he came upon the border village where Suppadevi had stayed. There, as was his wont, he pillaged and destroyed everything in sight, until those dwelling there were forced to flee.

These folk came to the army, lamenting that a lion had ravaged their homes. But none of the soldiers who went to stop him was able to stand up to the behemoth. The people then sent their demands to the king, pleading that he send a champion to end the creature's rampage.

The king of Vanga sent out a proclamation.

A noble elephant decked in rare fineries and bearing a thousand pieces of gold was led around the city. Men in royal livery marshalled the elephant and encouraged the heroes of the land to assemble in His Majesty's name. The first one to despatch the border beast to its Maker would receive the elephant and its burdens as a reward. 'Let him but promise to bring the head of the lion and all these are his to receive!' they cried.

Simhabahu heard the proclamation and ran to his mother crying that he would take the reward and kill the lion. A shocked Suppadevi forbade him to do so. Though he was an outlaw, a thief, murderer and despoiler of the worst manner, he was still Simhabahu's father, the one who had protected and sustained them all for over sixteen years.

Simhabahu remembered only a beast of the forest that had trapped them and caused him to lose his childhood. Every day he saw the charm, the variety of the world around him, and resentment for all he had missed clouded his mind. When he saw that his mother could not be coaxed or convinced in any way, Simhabahu made peace with her. Then, without telling his mother, he took the thousand gold pieces for slaying his own father.

The town criers presented the teenager to the king as the champion-to-be. Something about the boy moved the old king. Having no heir of his own, he promised the lad: *Slay the lion and I shall make you crown prince of this land.*

A delighted Simhabahu made his way back to the Lada forests. He tracked down the prison of his childhood. The mouth of the cave yawned before him and the boy, for all his ambition, quailed at the sight and hesitated from entering. Just then, a wail came from within – the lion. Recognizing his son at the entrance, the weary creature came forward, arms open to embrace his beloved child.

Simhabahu drew his bow and shot an arrow at his father. Three times did the young man shoot at his sire, but each time his strength failed in the grip of his conscience and the arrows bounced off his opponent's tough hide. The attacks finally drew the lion's wrath and he leapt towards the boy in blind rage.

This time, sensing that his life was on the line, Simhabahu drew with all his might and let go the arrow at the pouncing lion. The arrow pierced his father's body and the great beast fell dead in an instant.

Simhabahu lopped off the head with the great mane and returned to the city in triumph. He was welcomed joyfully by its citizens. In the seven days he had been away, the old king of Vanga had passed away. In accordance with his will, the ministers prostrated before the hero and begged him to be their king.

As the news of her son's adventures reached Suppadevi, she came rushing to his side. Many old courtiers recognized in delight and disbelief their long-lost princess. Simhabahu, revealed to be the old king's true grandson, was taken to the palace with much pomp and ceremony, and crowned the king of Vanga.

FOREIGN SHIPS IN LANKA

Vijaya, the eldest son of Simhabahu, was as leonine as his royal heritage demanded.

His parents encouraged him, indulged him, and entrusted his education to teachers of strategies, ethics and martial arts. Vijaya became a fine leader, but the men he chose to befriend were creatures of great mischief and few morals. In their company, the prince grew conscienceless and cruel. With time, their gang swelled in numbers and in violence, terrorizing the capital and its neighbourhood.

Simhabahu saw in his son the same reckless spirit that had led him, in his youth, to act without thought or fear of consequence. Just as his mother had failed to reason with him, he too could not make his son change his ways.

Vijaya appeased his parents with words but little curbed his activities once their backs were turned.

A day came when the people, despairing, flocked to the royal gates with a litany of crimes committed by the heir. They barged into the court and cried to their king:

> 'Time and time again, the crown prince and his associates have tested the justice of our kingdom of Lada. Each time, the officers, administrators and judges have set them above the law. Their criminal boldness grows day by day as they rob, kidnap and murder freely across the state. Who will remedy our grievances? Hear us now – if the king does not give us a way to live, we shall leave this land uncultivated, we shall leave the trade routes empty and we shall hand over the city to the forest. For if Lada follows the laws of the jungle, then let the jungle have Lada!
>
> 'However, if the officers and courts, under Your Majesty's command, give us justice and a means of living, we may then cultivate our lands, ply our trade and support all taxes and laws in the country.'

Simhabahu stood before his irate subjects and spoke persuasively. He made generous restitutions and promised the prince would be punished. But as the days passed, there was no sign of any disciplinary measures against the prince, who continued his debauchery and pillaging unchecked.

An enraged citizenry finally took up arms and barricaded the palace, demanding Vijaya's execution. Simhabahu would not war against his people, yet the memory of killing his father stopped him from executing his son. In the end, he exiled the boy and his villainous accomplices.

Before the jeering public, Vijaya and seven hundred of his followers had their heads half shaven. Half the beard and half the moustache were also razed off every condemned man's face. All the while, the people hooted, mocked and threw stones at them. The criminals were then put aboard a ship and cast out to sea. In two other vessels, the women and children of the outlaws were sent forth. As the sails receded to the horizon, the folk of Lada cheered and rejoiced to be rid of the horrific gang – and then they went home.

For uncountable days, the ships were thrown about on the sea. The sun rose and then the moon, wheeling across the sky in an endless churn. The clouds swept down and the waves swept up, walling them in a formless grey-blue. They were imprisoned in boundless repetition. What changed was only food and spirits — and these began to run low.

When all hope seemed lost, Vijaya's shipmates sighted a solid smudge in the distance. With the desperation of men fleeing a nightmare, they angled their vessel towards it. Land came into view, green and welcoming. With excitement and relief, the crew sailed into a shallow harbour. They flung themselves upon the sands, adding tears of joy to the salty shore. The other ships followed and the families were soon reunited. Now they turned their steps landwards, ready to tackle their new home.

Along the beach, they came unexpectedly upon an ascetic seated at the foot of a tree. Vijaya's men went to him and asked, 'Good sir, what place is this?'

'The island of Lanka,' he replied. 'Be at ease, for there is no danger to you here.'

They questioned him further, but the sage would not reply. He sprinkled water on them from his bowl and wound a thread about their hands. They thanked him for the blessing and then he left.

The exiles began to form bands to explore the land. A dog appeared before them, friendly but a little wary of the strangers. He appeared healthy and well looked after.

'Where there is such a tame creature, there are bound to be a civil people.' So saying, one of the men followed the animal as it gambolled inland.

Vijaya called after him, 'Take arms with you, for we do not know what welcome we will receive!'

His companion was already disappearing into the forests beyond the beach. Vijaya's men assuaged his concerns, reminding him of the what the sage had said and that they were guarded by his blessing.

Meanwhile, the scout pushed past screens of broad leaves and great tangles of roots, tracking his playful guide closely. He saw a wonderment of fruit and herbs, and gathered up the ripest treats in a knotted bundle for his children back on the beach. The trees suddenly gave way to a clearing. At its centre was a pond.

He stood mesmerized by its clear waters, gently rippling in the breeze. After the long sea journey, the fresh water held his attention with hypnotic force. He stumbled in his haste to get to it, fell to his belly and drank deep. Then, he crawled into the cool waters and bathed. When he was refreshed, he began gathering lotus shoots.

An outraged female voice filtered through to his ears, 'Stay! Thief! How dare you enter my estate without permission. Loot my harvest, foul my pond? Thief, I say, stop or *you will pay*!'

The man snorted derisively. He walked out of the water, gathered up the fruit and turned to leave. Putting her threat to action, the young woman stalked after him and caught him up by the ankle. He went down like a seesaw and smashed his nose on the ground. She dragged him along like a toy, leaving a thin trail of blood, to a nearby cliff. Poised on its edge, she swung him round twice and hurled him into the chasm. The unlucky villain landed in a swampy bed of greenery, injured and effectively imprisoned.

When their comrade did not return, the men on the beach ventured down the same path to discover his whereabouts. Some went alone and some in groups. So blindly did they believe in the ascetic's blessings that none planned for danger. And none of them returned to the beach. The damsel by the pond overpowered each of the seven hundred and confined them all to the chasm. At last, only Vijaya was left.

Knowing not what he was about to face, but certain that it was something deadly, he carefully armed himself. He chose five weapons for offence and defence – a bow, a battleaxe, a long sword, a spear and a hefty shield. Bristling and alert, he set out.

Soon, he came upon the pond as it lay twinkling under the noon-day sun. He ignored the temptation. Instead, he carefully scanned the area from canopy to ground. His eyes fell on a woman. She lay belly down, seemingly asleep, on a hammock.

Vijaya watched her for a while. She was dark-skinned with powerful limbs stretched in abandon like a slumbering panther. Her washed locks fanned out over the hammock and fell to the earth, dripping water.

Raising his battleaxe, he leapt forward, seized her by the hair and brought the blade just over her throat. The woman was startled awake and fought by instinct. But Vijaya had the advantage and held fast.

'Where are my men?' he demanded.

'Let me go! You have come a long way, from the look of you. Drink first and bathe. Then we may speak.'

'Where. Are. My. Men!'

'What do you want with those weak, uncouth men, a prince like you!'

Amazed to be recognized in such manner, Vijaya let her go. In a flash, he realized his error. As his enemy prepared to pounce, he drew his bow. The glint of the iron-tipped arrow made her pause.

'Slave!' Vijaya cried, 'Return my men at once and I will give you a merciful death!'

'No! Spare my life, sir!' cried the woman, falling to her knees. She looked up calculatingly. 'Spare my life and I will give you a kingdom in return.'

'You lie!' he growled. 'Where in this forsaken land is there a kingdom?'

'It is the truth!' she insisted. 'I am Kuveni, a Yakkhini. My people rule this rich land, but you do not see it for we are fast and lithe, and know how to be invisible to ordinary men. Still, I can show it all to you – and you will see how well we live, what incredible treasures we hold. If you let me go, I shall reveal to you and your men how to fight against my people… and how to win.'

'How do I know you will not betray us? You, who have vanquished seven hundred able-bodied men!'

'Let me live and I will swear by the gods to spend my whole life in your service. I will obey your every word.'

Vijaya lowered his bow cautiously. After all, his people needed a way to survive. 'Swear to me now,' he commanded and Kuveni swore allegiance to him. She then brought his men back and nursed their wounds.

When Vijaya said, 'They are hungry', she brought forth grains, edible roots, ripe fruit and sweet coconut water. When he said, 'They wish to rest', she showed them how to raise shelters and gave them goods for comfort.

She gave the prince gold and precious ornaments, adorning him in a royal manner. And she built for him a magnificent bed, canopied and secluded. The opulence and the heartfelt service of Kuveni delighted Vijaya and he made her his wife that very day.

By nightfall, the clan of seven hundred had erected sturdy tents on Kuveni's vast estate. They fell asleep as if dead to the world. As the fires died down and the stars became the sole source of light, the gentle island breeze wafted distant sounds of music and merriment towards the new encampment. It filtered through Vijaya's dreams and woke him up.

Turning to Kuveni, he asked, 'Where does this noise come from? Who's behind it?'

'They are the Yakkhas,' she told him, 'the people of this island. They are powerful and swift, so much so that many consider them invisible.

'Close by is their city of Sirisavatthu. The daughter of the Yakkha chief has come here from the capital city with her mother and a large band. They are celebrating the girl's wedding. For this, they will feast seven days. A great multitude has gathered and what we hear are the sounds of their celebrations.

'Before the high feast is over, you and your men must destroy the Yakkhas. Or else, it will never be possible for you to gain their kingdom.'

Vijaya was baffled. 'How can I slay the Yakkhas who are invisible?'

She replied, 'Be assured, I will help you slay them and become king of the island as I have promised. But you, my lord, must destroy every one of them, or else those who escape will turn on me. When they know that your men have gained a foothold in Lanka through my aid, they will kill me for it.'

'What is your plan, then?' asked Vijaya.

'Since you cannot see them, you must move to sound. I, who can see them, will track each body and utter a cry close to it at the right time. When you hear that signal, strike in its direction!'

Thus it was that the outcasts followed Kuveni to slaughter the revellers while they had their guard down.

The main nobility, the scholars and the warriors high of Lanka had gathered at the prestigious event. All lost their lives in the space of a night.

Vijaya stood over the bodies of the slain and rejoiced. He put on the garments of the Yakkha king and granted the noble raiment of other Yakkhas to his followers. In one fell swoop, he had taken over the island.

The seven hundred families got to work. As they days went by, they erected many settlements that grew into the cities of Lanka.

The place where they first landed and rested their weary bodies became the city of Tambapanni, for its red earth marked their palms as they rested, and their word for red hands was Tambapanni. Vijaya's men became ministers who lay the foundations of other cities. Anuradhagama was built by a man of that name near the River Kadamba. To this city's north, the priest Upatissa built Upatissagama on the banks of the River Gambhira. Three other ministers built, each for himself, Ujjeni, Uruvela and the city of Vijita.

The men, who once had been criminals, now turned into pillars of the state. Having faced the law so many times, they were familiar with it and put it to good use on their island. Vijaya and Kuveni ruled with a firm hand

and there was little crime to trouble them in these busy, early days of construction.

As all of them followed Vijaya, the son of King Simhabahu the lion-slayer, the people came to be called Sinhala. It was not long before they clamoured that Vijaya should undergo the formal rites that would make him king according to the scriptures. For they were no longer criminals but instead a civilized society of great achievements. They needed to raise their stature from shamed exiles to ministers of a legitimate court.

'Sire,' they said, 'consent to be consecrated as our king.'

Together the ruler and his closest coterie studied what was needed to make Vijaya a true king. They learned that unless a princess from a noble house became the queen, the prince could not be raised to the position of king.

Many tried to set this rule aside, but Vijaya firmly refused to proceed unless all rituals were performed by the book. Setting their minds to the issue, the ministers came up with a solution.

They recommended to Vijaya that an ambassador be despatched to the Pandyan king in the city of Madurai. That a fitting treasure of betrothal gifts of precious silks, jewels, pearls and other items be sent to him with this proposition: an alliance with the Sinhalese, to be made through marriage with a Pandyan princess for the prince and daughters of noble families for the ministers.

Vijaya acquiesced, and messengers were quickly sent forth to Madurai on ships laden with gifts. The Pandyan king, pleased with the offer and eager to spread his power to a new world, agreed to send a princess to Lanka. He also advised his ministers to send their daughters, and further sent a proclamation with the beat of a drum: 'Those men who are willing to let a daughter depart for Lanka shall provide their daughters with a double store of clothing and place them at the doors of their houses. By this sign shall we know that they are prepared to undertake the journey.'

A hundred maidens were thus brought out of their families and into the palace. The ruler acknowledged their contributions to the mission with weighty gifts.

He sent his own daughter, decked in expensive silks and ornaments, with all that was needful for the journey. The other maidens were outfitted as befit their rank. Elephants, horses and wagons heavy with dowries accompanied the girls. There were also craftsmen and a thousand families from eighteen different guilds.

In this manner, the wily Pandya hoped to acquire a tributary land for his dynasty – not through military might, but through the spread of his kingdom's culture, crafts and people. This sparkling procession made the short sea voyage to Lanka and disembarked at a spot that became known as Mahatittha. They were welcomed with stately ceremony by the Sinhalese and began their journey to the capital.

When news came to Vijaya that the ships from Madurai had arrived, he knew the time had come to deal with Kuveni – she who was now mother to their son and daughter. Knowing not how she might respond, he half coaxed, half threatened her.

'You, my most beloved one, who have vowed to follow my every word, I give you this last command. Leave this place, dear one. All men are fearful of superhuman beings. And they may seek to remove you – or worse, bring you down. You must see that these maidens must take precedence in our kingdom. This is no longer a suitable place for a Yakkhini. Leave, but leave behind our two children, for their own sakes and for the part they yet have to play.'

'Leave?' cried Kuveni. 'And where shall I go? This island has been my home long before you ever set foot on it. In your cities, who will shelter one whom the king has abandoned? And shall I sally back to what is left of my own people, so they may murder me?'

Vijaya spoke as if he had not heard. 'Delay not!' he urged. 'I will give you a thousand pieces of gold that you may go and live where you choose.'

She besought him again and again, but in vain. In anger, she left. She took her children and sought out her uncle, hoping that he would help her make peace with the remaining Yakkhas.

When she reached the Yakkha city, she hid her children on the outskirts, disguised herself and entered the city alone. Locating her uncle at his estate, she revealed herself, narrated her tale and begged for mercy.

Unknown to her, she was spotted by the Yakkhas on the estate. They recognized Kuveni and feared that she had come to spy on them for Vijaya. News of her presence rippled through the city and a mob rose to capture her. Kuveni fled, but they caught her. In that moment of rage and violence, they beat her to death.

Her uncle hurried from the city and sought out her children. 'My poor ones,' he exclaimed, 'if that crowd finds you, they will not spare you either. Therefore, be gone swiftly!' With no surety in their father's home and outright malice in their mother's, the children had nowhere to turn to in Lanka. They took their chance with the sea and set sail, away from the land of their parents.

Vijaya married the princess of Madurai and ruled for thirty-eight years. But he never again had children of his own. As he grew older, this weighed upon him. Without his family, the days seem to meld into each other and grew uncountable. He sometimes felt no different than on those days long gone by when he was thrown about untethered on the sea. The sun rose and then the moon, wheeling across the sky in an endless routine. His mind was awash with memories behind a wall of regrets. 'I am old and there lives no son of mine,' he grieved even as he died. For all his flaws, historians recorded that Vijaya was a peace-loving and righteous king.

DIDDA AND THE CROWN OF KASHMIR

The queen reclined on a divan in her fragrant garden. Tunga rested at her feet, his head upon her knees. She stroked his head languidly and stared at the fat moon in the night sky, near hypnotized by the halo of wispy gold circling the glowing orb with its faint smudges.

'It looks just like the king's pyre,' she mused. 'A great corona of flames, fair like the pale wives who threw themselves upon it, and a little smirched from the soot and ashes.'

Tunga the giant raised his head and followed her gaze. Then, he lifted a cup of wine to her, saying, 'It was a long time ago, madam. Many moons have passed since then.'

Didda took the proffered cup, tossed back its contents and felt the spirit burn down her throat.

'Even this,' she stared at the empty vessel, 'today, reminds me of that fire.' She smiled and handed it back to Tunga.

'All his wives committed sati,' she continued. 'In the end, I alone was left. The great all-engulfing blaze, the screams of departing women, the chanting priests, I hear them all ringing in my ears as if I were still there.'

Crickets chirped and clouds drifted across the horizon. The night was fresh and the breeze caressing. Yet, Tunga saw flames leaping in the queen's eyes. He blinked and the illusion was gone. Perspiration bloomed on her brow. He gently dabbed it, but Didda was many years away and did not notice.

'Abhimanyu, my beautiful lotus-eyed boy, was standing beside the prime minister,' she continued. 'That wily Phalguna! Do I miss him now that he's dead, ha! I made a show of seeking sati and that wicked man actually *permitted it*. Me! Join the others in immolation! As mother of the new king, and a child-king at that, I could have simply claimed my right to be regent.'

'No one would have stood in your way either,' said Tunga loyally.

'Certainly not!' preened Didda. 'Even when Kshemagupta was alive, he rarely took his duties to heart. The people looked to me, the daughter and granddaughter of proven kings, for decisions. The very coins minted in that time bore my syllable *Di* and the people were calling their ruler Didda-Kshema! And still that man felt no shame, not enough to mend his ways at least.'

Her husband had pursued excessive pleasures throughout his life – a predictably short one. He had returned from one of his many hunting expeditions with a high fever. Didda recalled how he had tossed and turned in bed, shrieking about she-jackals that spat flames at him. His body erupted in pustules that split and clotted like overcooked lentils. In less than a fortnight, he was dead. And soon, his corpse was set afire for real.

'But it was better to have the counsellors beg me to be regent.'

'How could you take such a chance? What if they hadn't stopped you?'

Didda's eyes gleamed.

'Foolish! Would I gamble my life upon so flimsy a hope as the support of men?'

Tunga glowered from beneath his ferocious brows and nipped her fingers. 'I am a man. I would give my life for you! Do you doubt it?'

'Had you been there, you would have sprung to my rescue at once… and spoiled all my plans!' she teased. 'But you were not there, Tunga,' she reminisced, falling back into her trance. 'And those who were, were content to have me stand in line before the piling corpses. I was so close to burning, my skin peeled back from the radiating heat. Abhimanyu's eyes were red, whether from the smoke of his father's pyre or from despair over his mother's impending death, I do not know. All about him stood sharp-eyed counsellors and mighty-limbed war veterans.

'It was at this last moment that two greybeards walked over to my side.

'Narvaahana, my old champion – he always spoke of the long strife that ended when I came to power. Those terrible years in which quarrelsome men rose, some ruling less than a year, and none outlasting a decade. To him, I was stability, peace, prosperity. A proven ruler. How could he give that up for a child-king, so prone to being torn apart by factions and likely as not poisoned or stabbed before he even graduated from his *gurukul?*

'Narvaahana blocked my way.

'In his booming baritone, he demanded, "Madam, we beg you once more to save yourself. Consider the need of the kingdom. Consider your people. More than all, consider the young king, who still requires your steady influence."

'I struggled not to show relief. No. Instead, I took a deep breath and insisted on committing sati!

'Twice more Narvaahana begged me to reconsider and twice more did I refuse. Our charade might have gone on for a while, had not commander-in-chief Rakka stepped up.

'Rakka too wanted me alive. But not for loyalty, oh no. Like me, he despised Phalguna and yearned to bring down that prime minister.

'"My queen," he said, "the time has not yet come to follow your husband. Look behind you at young lord Abhimanyu. Can you bear to leave such a tender one in such troubled times? Think you, will it be a year or less before some dastardly jackal usurps the throne?"

'His voice, long accustomed to bellowing over the din of battlefields, fell upon many ears. Many eyes turned upon Phalguna, whose hand lay on my boy's head. Ha! It was a sight, I tell you. The prime minister's eyes turned red, his nostrils flared, and, in the haze, he seemed to breathe smoke and flames upon us like a beast.

'Before such a terrifying sight, others cried out for me to stay, to rule, to guide Abhimanyu.'

The queen sighed. Her head lolled back on the silk cushions.

'Alas, that I should have outlived my beloved boy. I care not about the king's pyre. But how many, many moons it has been since Abhimanyu too joined his father. He who won the hearts of scholars and warriors alike. What better king could there have been?'

From the distance, clattering footsteps and loud pleading voices disturbed Didda's reminiscence.

'Your Highness, no! Please forbear! The queen must not be disturbed!'

Tunga sprang to his feet and placed his tremendous frame between the queen and the commotion. Into the lamplit garden strode the young King Bhimagupta.

Tunga relaxed a little, stepped aside and bowed to the child-king.

Didda noticed the boy trembling, but refrained from comment. She waited. The silence stretched on as he clearly struggled with his emotions. He then bent down stiffly, touched her feet and said, 'Grandmother!'

'Rise, dear one!' replied Didda, her smooth voice conveying all the affection of a snake to its hatchling. 'The hour is early yet for greetings. What urgent matter sends you barging past my guards?'

At this, the red-faced lad exploded. 'Such things have I overheard today, such whispers... I would not believe them.'

He glared at Tunga. 'But now I see that they are true!' he spat. 'You! How dare you!... an upstart herdsman... in the royal palace at this hour! What purpose... no, what permission do you have to be here? But what else can one expect from an uncouth nobody!'

'And you, most noble madam,' he narrowed accusing eyes on the queen, 'you who are the beacon we look to for guidance. You who are the pinnacle of our high kingdom. How can you? The daughter of kings and a widow, no less! If you but heard what is being said about... throw him out, I beg you. Send him back to his wild hut and his coarse sheep.'

His eyes met Didda's and his words dried up under the heat of her glare.

'What a fool have I bred!' she hissed, her face flushing darker and darker. 'To preach to *me* of morals and permissions? So, you heard words. What reply did you make? Or did you tuck tail and scuttle into your grandmother's chambers for a few sharp words? So easily driven about by his men! Who is the sheep and who the shepherd here?'

'What is wrong, is wrong!' Bhima cried, unheeding. 'And they are *not wrong*! It is your own teaching that tells me I must remonstrate. This arrogant peasant flaunts how he has your favour and no one can say a word to him. He has filled the halls with his low-born brothers and they strut about before high-ranking ministers. Not satisfied with that, they have wrested power from experienced bureaucrats, men of ancient lineage and proven service! They hire mercenaries to threaten the people and strong-arm...'

'Cease!' commanded Didda.

Bhima came to a halt, his breathing harsh and laboured.

'Guards!'

Two men shimmered in from the gloaming.

'His *Majesty* is drunk and unaware of what he says. Take him to his chambers! Bathe his head in cold water until he comes to his senses.'

The guards made to take Bhima's arm, but he shook them off. He cast a last accusing look at the queen and stalked off.

Didda looked after him disgustedly. 'How did such a bright and high-minded boy as my Abhimanyu beget such an unthinking, unrestrained fool of a son.'

'He is king and he wishes to rule,' shrugged Tunga. 'It is natural that he would use the old aristocracy to bring pressure on you and cause a rift between us.'

'No, it is the old aristocrats who use him. They must be getting desperate, with so many new faces taking power at court. They cannot stop me from ennobling whom I wish, so they twist the boy to their purpose.'

Tunga face turned smug. 'It's a pity then, that the young hothead is of so little use to them. What will they do now that their budding king is under lock and key?'

'Remain alert, love,' said the queen. 'Those wily foxes are ever eyeing the lion's seat. And too many have climbed on to it successfully.'

'Your loyal dogs shall hunt them all down,' grinned Tunga. 'Would you care for a coat made of their skins this winter? Keep you warm.'

Didda laughed.

Word spread that the young king was confined in a terrible place of cold stone and rusted iron, on icy water and mouldy scraps, until he bent his will to the regent's commands.

When Abhimanyu had died young, the queen's grief had been evident. The people sympathized with her. Her grandson took the throne, passed away and the people were shocked by their bad luck. A second grandson was crowned. When he died, whispers began that the queen wished to keep power. No evidence of foul play came up, *so was she using witchcraft?* they wondered.

Now the last son of the direct line of Kshemagupta seemed under threat. The noises began to grow.

Many forces sided with the queen, for she had ruled a long time and held the kingdom in the palm of her hand. Many who had lost her favour or hoped to gain elsewhere, clamoured to see the young king. When he failed to show up, they wailed that Bhima was, in fact, dead.

Yet, no cause can survive without a figurehead. And so, they revived him with a fresh tale: that the Bhima who had died in the dungeons was not the true Bhima.

Abhimanyu's wife, they said, feared her imperious mother-in-law, and early on, swapped her youngest son with the boy of a noble house. When Didda discovered this deception, she imprisoned the false Bhima and quietly took care of him. Now where was the true king?

Children in the street found a favourite new rhyme. They were seen skipping to it:

The cuckoo in the crow's quarters,
has *splat!* the crow's eggs flung;
The Timi-fish in sacred waters,
has gobbled its own young;

Yet, the Timi is called a sage.
And can a crow live to old age?

Events came to a head when the kingdom's Brahmins banded together. They flooded into the capital, crowding its squares, avenues and *dharamshalas*. They would fast, they said, until answers were given. The citizens saw these men wilting by the waysides and grew upset.

When the queen remained silent, great multitudes followed the Brahmins to the royal gates. They demanded for Tunga to be sent out that he may answer for the crimes of overpowering the ruler and leading the regent astray.

Within the castle, an enraged Tunga called for his armour and horse to be prepared. Before he could set out, Didda swept into the hall.

'Stop,' she ordered.

'Till they break in and seize you?' demanded Tunga.

'They will not harm me. Do you not hear them? It is *you* they want.'

'For a group that's been fasting, they sure are gutsy,' Tunga growled. 'Command us to take them down. We'll have them swinging by their innards!'

'They are my own people. You will not harm them!'

'Then what is your plan?'

'First, you must leave.'

'What?!' roared Tunga.

'This way. There is no time for debate. Obey me!'

Tunga nevertheless debated heatedly. 'Would you have me run from a fight? Should I behave like the very knave they all call me?'

Didda caught him by the scruff of his neck and pulled him down till he was at eye level.

'Obey me,' the queen said evenly, her gaze narrow and calculating.

Tunga grunted but put up no further protests. 'What is your plan?' he asked again as the attendants ushered him out of the room.

'Tell him,' Didda waved to her attendants as she swept off in the opposite direction.

'General,' said one of the counsellors, 'the queen wishes you to fight elsewhere.'

'The ruler of Rajapuri, the mighty Prithvipala, has watched the guardians of our land split into factions and clash with each other. He has now sallied into the weakest territories, harassing and overpowering the most vulnerable lords and their lands.

'In anger, these ministers assembled an expedition to go against him. The queen permitted it, but Prithvipala has attacked our forces and all but destroyed them. Many old ministers have lost their lives and others have fallen into deep distress.'

'Serves them right for troubling the queen so!' grumbled Tunga.

'The queen commands you and your brothers to wrest her lands, imprisoned warriors and noblemen back from Prithvipala.'

Tunga threw back his head, delighted. 'How wonderful to see their faces when this low-born shepherd comes to their rescue! Let us be off then!'

Meanwhile, Didda walked down the castle ramparts, followed by only a handful of armed guards. When she stood over the gates, horns blared to announce her presence and the rabble squinted upwards. She stood above them, grey-haired and straight-backed, her robes flapping in the wind, the very picture of a stern mother.

'My people are always welcome in my castle,' she cried. 'Especially you well-beloved, who have shown such care and concern for our person. Advisers within have asked us to open the gates and send forth the fort's forces.'

Many in the crowd blanched.

'But fear not those old and troublesome counsellors. If we open the gates, it will be only to invite you in.'

She smiled up and down the crowd and every man felt singled out by that unnerving gaze.

'I will open the gates now. Those who wish to come in and speak with me will be given safe passage. The rest of you, go home and wait for the outcome of our discussion. No one shall remain at the gates. Choose – either in or out!'

With that, she turned and strode back in. Men-at-arms began to appear on the ramparts. More filled the courtyard below. Stone-faced, they lifted the gates and waited. The group took counsel and split in two – one melted away into the city and the other, a group of Brahmins, made their way into the fort. The queen's attendants guided them to the audience chamber.

It was the start of a long-drawn negotiation. The Brahmins represented the old aristocrats and held much sway over the people. Didda lay innumerable arguments before them. Day after day, she spoke to them of the advantages of a steady rule as Narvaahana had once laid them before her. Not least, she lay before them great piles of gifts and gold.

The Brahmins largely surrendered to her special blend of power, praise and presents. Not only did they end their fast, but no mention was made of the missing boy-king. One point alone remained – she demanded to be crowned in her own right, not just to rule in the name of yet another puppet male.

As this delicate detail was being brokered, a military courier was ushered into the audience chamber. He gave his news to the queen, and she was pleased to have him announce it to the others.

Turning to the assembly, the rider spoke his message word for word as it was given to him, 'This humble Tunga, your ever loyal and most devoted servant, greets Your Majesty on the auspicious occasion of victory. The king of Rajapuri has thrown down his arms and surrendered before your forces. Even now, my brothers are liberating our nobility from his camps. In the meanwhile, your newest servant Prithvipala has offered rich tribute, which I am entrusting to this faithful courier.'

The congregation absorbed this in silence, then erupted in cheers. To have subdued so clever and bold a rival as Prithvipala! And to have shown such mercy to the old nobles, the very men who tried to oust her when they should have been her loyal ministers. The scholars raised their voice to praise Didda's magnanimity and blessed her with a long reign. When the hubbub died, the matter of who would sit on Kashmir's throne was settled.

Bhima was, indeed, dead. Official records did not say how. A coronation was held for Didda and she became queen in act and fact.

On a fair day, the ageing ruler arranged for her nephews to play in the royal gardens. When all were gathered, her servant flung great baskets of apples all around. Didda spoke to the princes, 'Shall we see how many of these apples you can gather? The one who gets the most will be mightily rewarded!'

A fierce sport ensued. Clothes were rent and great bruises were born as the princes dove for the apples on the ground and across each other's bodies.

In the end, the clear winner was Samgramaraja, the son of Didda's brother.

She saw his unblemished clothes, his clean hands and face, his unruffled hair and asked, 'How did you gather so many apples without getting into a fight?'

He answered, 'I got the fruit by making those boys fight furiously with one another. I stood apart until they tired themselves battling it out. What success may not fall to those who stand alert with a cool mind while those of unrestrained passions burn themselves out?'

Didda remembered her grandson who had so easily been manipulated by others. How different was this astute and collected youth in front of her. Didda adopted Samgramaraja, and in doing so, gave Kashmir a ruler who held its borders securely against an ambitious host of invaders.

THE LOST TREASURE OF BIMBISARA

Bimbisara, the youthful ruler of Magadha, was idly watching the river flow by when his attention was snared by an ascetic walking along the near bank. The man was gaunt – as you would expect of a hermit – but he was also boyish in face, clean in habit, and strode with energy and purpose.

'Who is that?' Bimbisara asked his attendants.

They followed their master's gaze to the distant figure and answered, 'There goes one who is much praised by men and women, young and old alike. He has many names, sire. We call him Gautama. Once he was called Prince Siddhartha, son of King Suddhodhana of the Shakya people.'

Others in the retinue agreed. 'Indeed, he has such thoughtful manners, speaks without the arrogance of other sages and is so full of grace in expression and action, that all who see him are happy and freely give him alms.'

Bimbisara sent forth a messenger to bring him the man.

The sage drew up to the king's seat and faced him equably, unfazed by the grandeur of the site or the occasion. Never before had anyone faced Bimbisara with such equanimity and he was much struck by it.

'Royal cousin,' he exclaimed, 'great destiny is writ upon your brow. Why have you it left it behind to don this hermit's garb?'

The sage smiled and softly replied, 'I was Siddhartha, born a prince of the Shakyas. But now I have renounced the world and people call me only Shakyamuni. To fulfil the fate that you speak of, I cannot tie myself to any court, place or person.'

Dissatisfied with this reply, the king tried again, 'Gautama, your father has long been our friend. Have you quarrelled with him? Are unable to go back? If so, stay here and I shall give you half my kingdom. What do you say?'

Gautama replied, 'Sir, I have no quarrel with anyone. I love my family – my parents, my wife and son, and everybody. I wish only to find a way to stop old age, sickness, worry and death. So I cannot stay in this or any other court. For your noble offer I thank you, but I must leave all the same.'

No matter how he coaxed, Bimbisara could not stay the *muni*. However, he managed to extract a promise that should Gautama ever find what he sought, he would return to the capital and to his new-found friend.

With that, the two men parted ways.

As time went by, Siddhartha pursued his spiritual goal, while Bimbisara sought more earthly gains.

King that he was, he set about expanding the borders of Magadha. But wishing to avoid bloodshed, he sought expansion by forming allies where he could avoid war.

He married three princesses and bound their powerful home countries to him. Through his marriage with Princess Chelana, the bountiful Himalayan state of Licchavi came under his influence. Through his marriage with Kosaladevi, the mighty King Pasendi of Kosala became his friend. Finally, his marriage to princess Kshema allied Magadha with the Madra kingdom.

Once, he learnt that his long-standing rival Pradyot, King of Avanti, was tortured by a 'yellowing' disease. Bimbisara sent over his own court physician. This brilliant doctor, Jivaka, cured Pradyot of his jaundice. The grateful king of Avanti, for this miracle cure, became a firm friend to Bimbisara.

With such deeds, Magadha became much favoured by its neighbours. As peace flourished, borders opened to trade and talent. His administration prospered, and Bimbisara grew rich and powerful.

In time, Siddhartha became Buddha, the Enlightened One. Executing his old promise, he journeyed to Magadha with his disciples. Bimbisara received him in Rajagriha, the capital city, with joy and honour. To ensure that the Buddha and his students were comfortable and would stay for years to come, the king gifted them his pleasure gardens, the enchanting Veluvana. Here, the

Buddha stayed for a long time and taught many who flocked to him for spiritual guidance.

Among the Buddha's disciples at Veluvana was his own cousin Devadatta. When Devadatta first became a follower, he was a clear-minded monk. But later, he grew arrogant, and seeing how the Buddha was feted and worshipped, he became jealous and covetous.

One day, in a gathering of students and princes, Devadatta spoke out against the Buddha.

'For too long have you been in charge,' he claimed. 'Step down and let someone else lead the *sangha*!' But the Buddha, with insight into his cousin's true motives, refused. Nor did anyone else take Devadatta's side.

Angered and humiliated before his fellow monks, Devadatta vowed to bring down the Buddha. *First,* he thought, *I must remove his most influential supporters*. That meant getting rid of the wise and powerful Bimbisara.

Devadatta began whispering false words to members of the *sangha*, promising them supernatural powers and shortcuts to high status. Those who lent an ear to such manipulation became his followers.

He then sought out warriors and princes who might be happy to take down Bimbisara. But most laughed him away or threw him out of their court.

One alone gave heed to his words. Ajatashatru, the ambitious son of Bimbisara and Chelana, allowed his mind to be poisoned against his father.

Devadatta whispered to him. 'My pitiful prince,' he purred, 'how dreadful it is to see one so powerful be so chained by circumstance. So worthy a scion, the noblest of all his blood, and yet your father does not acknowledge it. Or he would have proclaimed you crown prince by now.'

Ajatashatru's eyes flashed at these words.

'Mistake me not!' cried Devadatta. 'I merely say to your face what others are whispering among themselves. They would willingly have your guiding hand raised over them. Indeed, they have long expected it and are surprised to see that you do not stake your claim more boldly. How much longer will you let another pull the strings? Let another decide who will rise to the throne?'

Emotions warred in the prince's heart. On the one hand, his father was king. He had the right to command the princes and choose his successor. Surely, he would choose Ajatashatru. Or did he see Ajatashatru's popularity as a threat? Or did he perhaps favour another son? The king's mind was a mystery.

Devadatta added fuel to these inflamed thoughts. 'Is it not clear yet? If your father has not appointed you as his heir, it can only mean one thing... the crown of Magadha is destined for another brow.'

'Will you allow a white-haired man – powerful yes, but ageing fast... and, ah, quite clear in mind? – to stand between you and your birthright?

'Perhaps it will not be so bad. I myself have an illustrious brother in the Enlightened One. It is my blessing to bow before him! Will you be happy too, bowing before one of your brothers?'

Caught up in a maelstrom of conceit and doubt, Prince Ajatashatru plotted with gruesome intent.

One night, he strapped a dagger to his thigh and stole into his father's chambers. It was an ill-conceived act. For even as he crept towards the sleeping figure, a guard noticed the glint of movement.

'To the king! To the king!' he shouted and sprung upon the shadow by the bedside.

Bimbisara came to with a start and flung himself to one side. A swarm of guards burst into the chambers and bore down upon the tussling figures.

'Cease!' roared the king.

Instantly the fight stopped. The guards moved back – all but two, who held a crouching figure by its neck and arm, face firmly down.

'Lights!' flew the command, and 'Bring him here', in a voice shaking with anger.

As the lamps flared to life, the guard dragged the kneeling figure to the king's feet and lifted its head.

Bimbisara looked into the eyes of his son. His own widened in disbelief. Such murderous intent flickered in his boy's gaze. The king stumbled back into a couch.

'Take him back,' he said through gritted teeth. 'Keep him under close guard. And summon the court.'

Word of that night's misadventures spread rapidly among the ministers. They stood before the king long before dawn broke and he addressed them in the flickering gloom.

'My good advisers,' he began, 'too long have I been on this throne, to see such a day as this.'

The ministers fell to their knees and objected loudly.

'The prince must pay for his crime,' they shouted. 'He shows no remorse even now. Such an act cannot be forgiven. Sire, he must pay with his life and no less.'

Bimbisara raised his hands and the hubbub died down.

'Too long have I been on this throne, to see such a day as this,' he repeated, and no one spoke this time. 'My own father passed his crown to me when I was an adolescent. For all my achievements, I have shown but little of his wisdom. This must be rectified immediately.'

He rose and announced. 'Let preparations be made for the crowning of the prince!'

The court exploded in uproar. Not one would submit to such an announcement, but Bimbisara was adamant. In the days to come, he convinced his ministers one by one.

And so, setting Ajatashatru upon the throne, he went into retirement.

Devadatta was peeved. This was hardly the outcome he had hoped for. However, even in retirement, the old king held great sway. Devadatta took the opportunity to berate Ajatashatru.

'Who leaves a defeated king alive? The people love him as ever. As do the ministers, the generals and the priests. Even the neighbouring powers all worship him! Should he disagree with something you do, who will stand with you? Who would follow your word over his? Can you rule like this? And if he should ever change his mind... could you retain your throne against him?'

In a fit of panic, Ajatashatru set out after his father. Bimbisara was caught and thrown into the deepest and darkest of prisons.

He was allowed neither food nor visitor. Yet, Queen Chelana managed to visit and look after him. When news of this came to Ajatashatru, he ordered the guards to remove any dishes or clothes his mother brought with her. In desperation, Chelana covered her body in honey and ghee, and so fed Bimbisara. Every day, she tried to mend the bond between father and son.

'There was a time,' she told him, 'when you were in my womb and I was overcome with the desire to feed on a human heart. One of the princes fried a wild fruit that looked like meat and gave it to me. Later, I feared that this demonic act of mine – for I did not know then that it was just fruit – would make you, my son, a demon too. I became so convinced in this matter that as soon as my child was born, I threw him away in a garbage heap. And there you would have died, if it hadn't been for your father. When he discovered you gone, he forced the story out of me and ran to your rescue.

'He found you in the garbage dump and saw that a cock had bitten your finger. It had become infected and was bleeding. Unheeding, he, the king, put your finger in his mouth and sucked the pus and blood out. And he did so for days until your finger was healed.

'And you! To such a noble father, what have you done?'

With such stories as these, Chelana prevailed over her son. The fog lifted from Ajatashatru's mind.

Overcome with remorse and love for his father, he picked up a sturdy rod and rushed to the dungeons. He meant to break down the prison door, but Bimbisara saw a deranged man come running at him with an iron rod. Unwilling to be beaten to death, and in horror of what his son was about to commit, Bimbisara took his own life.

The news of the king's death spread rapidly through the palace. One of the royal ladies, in grief and horror at the turn of events, decided that Ajatashatru should never lay his hands on all that Bimbisara held. Knowing that the new king gloried in his ill-gotten gains, she decided he must suffer some punishment at least.

Under the cover of chaos, she made swift arrangements to cart away the vast treasure that Bimbisara had accumulated in his life. No one could hold such a hoard and be safe. The lady wisely donated it all to a Tirthankara. But what need does a Jain *muni* have for gold and glittering gems?

Along a cliff face, the men of his sect had carved grottoes in which to live and meditate. The sage took the valuables to one such cave and walled it up securely. Yet, word soon spread among thieves and plunderers of a *son bhandar* (golden hoard) in the vicinity. For years, they tried to get their hands on it. Centuries passed, and men brought cannons and gunpowder to break through the rock. Yet, the cannonballs shattered like coconuts against the stone, their forceful mark no more than a *tilak* on a broad forehead.

Though none have discovered Bimbisara's treasure, all who came to the cave found on its wall a message carved in a long-forgotten language. It is said that the cave will open only to one who can decipher the password.

THE FAVOURITE SON AND THE OTHER ONE

Devadatta was soaring in meditation, enraptured and boundless. He was completely unaware that a great foe was climbing up from darkest oblivion towards him. Clawing this way and that, it breached Devadatta's mind in the form of long-forgotten grudges. His memories crept up, casting unpleasant, unformed shadows. They writhed, spiked and coagulated into forms.

There he saw Siddhartha, his maternal cousin. They were both young, and fighting over a swan. Resentment boiled over as Devadatta witnessed, once more, his cousin walk away triumphant with the beautiful snow-white bird.

Now he saw Siddhartha, older, silhouetted against a gathering of monks. A halo seemed to surround him.

The shadows of great warrior kings stood tall in the diminishing light. They bent their knee to Siddhartha. Other shapes circled eagerly towards his figure. Scholars paid him homage and the great masses flocked like raucous birds, crying his praise.

Devadatta's mind flooded with the scents of divine gardens and incense-filled monasteries, all built to host Siddhartha, to tempt him to stay longer. The people yearned to be near him, hear his words and marvel at his teachings.

A sudden spasm sent bitter bile into the back of his mouth.

Disgusted, Devadatta spat and tried to clear his head. But his mind had other ideas. It wandered back to the days when he and Siddhartha competed as siblings, princes of the Shakya clan. In time, they both became monks. Both gained spiritual knowledge and the respect of their peers. Both were equally honourable. Were they not? The question seeped in unchecked.

Devadatta's memories paused at princess Yashodhara, first seeing her cheerful, then a forlorn figure with a babe in her arms. *He abandoned my sister.*

Visions rose of Siddhartha's son, Rahula, renouncing the world. *Then he took the boy!*

The monks, vying to get closer to the master. They all treat him like an infallible sage and chase after him. *Fools, can you not think for yourselves! How can you be so easily directed like witless sheep. And by such a man, who forsakes his family, abandons his duties as a prince, yet conquers kings and lands and sets himself above others.*

Devadatta opened his eyes and the green world, shrouded in afternoon silence, looked back at him. With sudden clarity, he realized the twisted path his mind was taking. It was mischievous and base. And though he knew that it baited him, he did not resist.

On that day, Gautama Buddha was in the midst of a large assembly. Gathered about him were princes, noblemen, pandits and numerous devotees. They were lost in the words of the Enlightened One as he expounded his beliefs. Devadatta strode into this illustrious crowd. No one noticed. He took a seat and cast his assessing gaze over the multitudes. He watched Gautama, watched the spellbound throng, watched even as his inner demons fed on rising jealousy and grew stronger by the passing minute.

When the Buddha paused in his speech, Devadatta strode forwards to gain his attention. He adjusted his robes, set a palm to his heart and spoke with engaging softness.

'O Blessed One, who has guided us these all-too-short years, the last phase of life is upon you. Elderly One, it is time for you to seek rest. Devote your days to preparing for the next step of your journey and lay down the heavy burdens of the *sangha*. There are many here who could take on the mantle. Indeed, and it be your wish, you may leave it safe in my hands and this humble one shall guide the brotherhood…'

'Stop, Devadatta!' interrupted the Buddha. 'The *sangha* shall not be yours. Give up the idea of taking charge here.'

Devadatta scowled but boldly turned towards the assembly and repeated himself.

'I appeal to the great lords assembled here. Join your pleas with mine. The Blessed One is advanced in age. He has long borne our cares and guided us. It is now our duty, our turn, to care for him. It is time to let him be at ease. The great responsibilities of the *sangha* ought to be with one who is energetic enough to handle its demanding tasks. And one who has known the Blessed One since childhood, and is well versed in his ways and words.

'As such,' he gestured at himself, 'is there any priest more qualified to guide the *sangha* henceforth?'

An astonished silence clung momentarily to the crowd. It gave way to a spiral of snickers and some shouts of outrage.

Behind him, Gautama spoke once more, 'I would not give the *sangha* even to one so capable as Saariputta or Moggallaana. Why, then, would I leave it to a miserable self-seeker like you, monk?'

The crowd cheered his words. Saariputta and Moggallaana stood up and bowed before their master. Devadatta felt his cheeks heat with shame. *Even before kings he does not hesitate to use such strong words,* he thought. *How can a holy man speak so and be worshipped still. Why for such a one did the heavens send omens at his birth?*

Outwardly, he bowed to Gautama as if acquiescing with the great sage and the will of the assembly. He circumambulated the Holy One and departed the grounds. Inwardly, his rage screamed at him to get even.

All the kings are dedicated followers of Gautama, he ruminated. *What chance do I stand against such powerful allies? Is there someone mightier who can stand at my side? Someone who can be turned into a faithful disciple to my every wish?*

His mind sorted through a list of possible candidates and focused on Prince Ajatashatru, the son of Bimbisara. The warrior-like youth had a reputation for being unruly and unheeding of his parents and advisers. Such an ambitious one, unrestrained by morals or a conscience, could be the very sword he needed to skewer his enemy. But Bimbisara, one of Gautama's most powerful supporters must go, and Ajatashatru placed on the throne.

Devadatta began plotting.

In time, Ajatashatru became king. His gratitude to Devadatta was so great, he would visit the monk with five hundred chariots, morning and evening! He donated, for Devadatta's sake, five hundred pots of food each day and indulged every whim the monk expressed. Devadatta rejoiced in his powerful new disciple and all the accompanying extravagance – much to the consternation of the *sangha*. The brotherhood murmured at his activities and wondered why the Buddha did not chastise him. Surely, this was not the right path for a member of the *sangha*!

There were other monks whose wonderings took a different turn. *How did Devadatta acquire the new king as a follower,* they asked. *He must have extraordinary powers to win over such an arrogant and terrifying prince. We should seek out Devadatta,* they decided. *If we learn from him, we too might become powerful.*

These men did not worry that Ajatashatru had become the ruler at Rajagriha using ignoble methods under Devadatta's tutelage. They opened their ears to his instruction and soon their minds were distracted from their true paths.

More and more began to join Devadatta's cause. When his followers numbered some five hundred, the Buddha sent Saariputta and Moggallaana to bring them back. These two men gathered the men who had wandered into Devadatta's net by promises of profit and power.

'Monks, do you set your expectations high, seeing Devadatta's gains?' they asked. 'Heed us, for he is not one who will benefit from them. Rather, they will lead to his destruction. The Enlightened One says, just as the banana fruit kills the banana plant and the bamboo fruit kills the bamboo plant, so also the gifts harvested by a corrupt man will see him to his end.'

These words shook the listeners. *Had they been wrong to seek shortcuts and quick gains?* All five hundred returned to the *sangha.*

Devadatta was furious. He had once more lost to his cousin. Ajatashatru too heard of this incident. Knowing that nothing would please his teacher more than Gautama's life, he gifted Devadatta a number of well-trained assassins.

Devadatta quickly set them to work. He chose one from among the men, held out a map to him and said plainly, 'Seek out this place where Gautama is now stationed in contemplation. When you see him, make sure no one from the monastery is nearby. Then take his life and escape by this other road here.'

The man nodded and left.

Devadatta then called two more assassins. 'Hide yourselves along this road,' he said to them, pointing to a spot along the first assassin's escape route. 'You will see a man coming from the direction of the monastery. Know that he is deadly with knife and sword. Do not engage him at close quarters, but pull out your arrows from your hiding place and shoot him on sight.'

After they were despatched, he ordered forth four more assassins. To them he said, 'Hide yourselves down the bend of this route. You will see two men coming round from the direction of the monastery. Know that they are masters of the blade and sword. Do not engage them at close quarters, but pull out your arrows from your hiding place and shoot them on sight. Be sure to leave no trace.'

Devadatta then set a group of eight men to kill these four assassins, and a group of sixteen to kill the last eight men. Thus he hoped to cover any tracks that could lead the murder of Gautama back to him.

The first killer strapped on a quiver, shouldered a bow and made his way to the arena where his prey was expected. Gautama, who had completed his meditations, was out for a walk. The assassin heard footsteps from his appointed place and warily drew his bow. As he took aim, anticipating the appearance of the monk on the path, his eyes fell upon a radiant being. A face of such serenity, a frame so noble, the thought of a crime against it was anathema. It caused the strength to leave his arm. He gazed upon the glowing figure and felt a compulsion to greet him. He abandoned his weapons, stumbled out of hiding and fell trembling across the Buddha's path.

When the Buddha laid a hand on his head, he confessed, 'I am an evil and foolish man, O Divine One.

I approached you with murder in mind but am now crushed by the enormity of my transgressions. May you forgive my evil ways and accept me as your servant.'

Further up the road, two assassins waited for their own mark. When no one turned up and the shadows grew longer, they came out of hiding. *What is taking him so long,* they wondered and went up the road to seek him out.

There they came across the Buddha seated under a tree, their target humbly at his feet. As with the first, so with this pair. Gautama's radiance took their breath away. When his eyes fell on them, their guilt screamed in their ears. In desperation, they sought refuge in the Blessed One and looked to him for instruction.

Soon they were joined by the four, the eight and the sixteen. All listened to the Buddha's words and returned submissive to Devadatta. 'O sage,' they said, 'it is beyond any of us to deprive Gautama, the Holy One, of his life.'

'Enough!' cried Devadatta, beside himself with rage. 'I shall do it myself!'

He spoke loud and unheedingly, and many monks heard his vile vow. They rushed to guard the Buddha, but the sage shooed them away saying, 'It is not so easy to kill me!'

Alone, Gautama trod the serene path in the shadow of Vulture's Peak. The gentle slope was shrouded by green and dry branches, silent but for the occasional chatter of monkeys and birds.

The calm was broken by a thunderous crash. The Buddha looked up and saw a boulder wrecking wood, soil and stone as it rolled down the granite hill. It was headed straight for him. Halfway down, it struck another rock and came to an abrupt standstill.

In the returning silence, dust and debris slid down the hillside. A splinter of stone flew all the way down and struck Gautama's foot. Blood oozed from the wound, but he seemed little bothered.

Instead, his eyes travelled high up, scanning the outcrops of rocks at the peak. He spied Devadatta, who was craning eagerly from the edge.

'Alas,' remarked the Buddha, pity lacing his words.

Devadatta drew back hastily. *Had he been seen?* Irate and embarrassed, he climbed down the hill, unsure what consequences he would be facing. He kicked at stones and struck out at tree trunks, raging against yet another failed plot.

A couple of mornings later, monks of the *sangha* were on their routine walk through the city, bowls in hand.

They knocked on door after door, begging for alms, and returned every donation of food and drink with blessings.

A hubbub at the end of one street caught their attention. Vendors, cleaners, pedestrians – even the dogs and crows – all turned as one when screams erupted in the distance. In no time at all, panicked citizens were streaming up the road.

'Run for your lives!' they shouted. 'A rogue elephant is on the loose!'

Fierce trumpeting rose above the shrieks and confirmed this fact. The monks hiked up their robes and took to their heels.

Up the street came the maddened mammoth, Naalagiri. For breakfast, she had been fed sixteen pots of alcohol. As she swayed from foot to foot, she found herself unexpectedly free of tethers. Taking the proffered opportunity, she exited the royal stables and was now having the time of her life in the market – although she found the scampering of these tiny two-legged creatures a little annoying.

She chased after the pitiful dwarfs, bowling some over and sending others flying through the air. In the midst of her merriment, she caught sight of a lone figure. It stood stock still in the madly spinning world.

Naalagiri gambolled towards it. Around her, monks were wailing at the figure, 'Turn back, O Blessed One! Turn back! The elephant has turned into a man-killer!

Lord, may you turn back now!' From the roofs and upper storeys, people screamed warnings and watched aghast as the elephant gained steadily upon Gautama.

He did not hear them, or gave no sign of it. His attention was fixed solely on the animal, and when he spoke, his voice was soothing and sonorous. His words were chanted liltingly. Naalagiri stopped flapping her ears, lowered her trunk and listed to the mellifluous verse:

'Elephant, don't harm one who is true –
Harming such a one is suffering to yourself;
For one who harms the innocent, elephant,
There is no rest to be found afterwards.

Be intoxicated no more; be heedless no more.
The heedless have no harbour at their journey's end.
Do only that by which you will reach a good destination.'

Speaking continuously in his low voice, the Buddha began to walk towards the palace. Mesmerized, Naalagiri followed. For weeks after, people sang of his glorious deed:

Some men tame with a rod,
With a goad or a whip;
But one whose will is sharper still?

The greet seer of Rajagriha –
His song makes monsters kneel.

Someone let it slip that the palace mahout had taken orders from Devadatta to set a drunk elephant rampaging. 'How evil is he,' they whispered, using the king's name to plot against Gautama. 'Oh, and how ill-fated: have you heard how his many disciples deserted him?' Even King Ajatashatru, with the weight of leadership firmly of his shoulders, repented and sought the Buddha for forgiveness.

When the erring ones returned to the fold, the Buddha told them a story.

'Monks,' he said, 'out in the wilderness, there lives a herd of elephants whose lives depend on a vast lake. Every day, the grand creatures dive into the waters. They pull up lotus roots and stalks, wash them carefully, and when the stalks are free of mud, chew and swallow the plants. This has given them beauty and power, and keeps them from both pain and death.

'In the herd are also young elephant calves. They mimic their wise elders, plunge into the lake and root out lotus roots and stalks. But unlike the old ones, they are not vigilant and do not wash the stalks well. Thus, when they chew, they swallow also a great deal of mud and dirt. This keeps from them both beauty and strength. For them, there is no relief from pain or death.

'In much the same way, monks, the wretched Devadatta, imitating me, will die.'

Indeed, Devadatta, distraught by his many failures and consumed by the foe within, fell ill. When repentance came at last to the fallen sage, it was too late – he died before he could fulfil his last wish of meeting the Buddha one final time.

In a strange twist of fate, he, who was so against the Buddha in life, helped save Buddhism after his death. Many hundreds of years later, Western missionaries sailed to Asia to spread the message of Christ. In Siam, people saw the figure of the cross and mistook it for Devadatta being impaled in the underworld for his many evil acts. The king believed this new religion came from Devadatta. He thus banned it from the state and his subjects remained staunchly Buddhist!

WINNER TAKES ALL

King Ajatashatru and the eagle-eyed Vassakaara frowned over the map before them.

A bold, undulating line across the tan leather marked the mighty Ganga. On the southern bank stretched their kingdom of Magadha. To the north lay Vaishali and the lands of the Licchavis.

A single town straddled the river, with its network of roads fanning out to both Magadha and Vaishali. It was called Pattanagama.

'These hills,' pointed Vassakaara, cutting an arc with his arm, 'and these. The Licchavis have been mining precious stones here. Not metals for weaponry like we originally thought. It's been a task getting past their guards, but our latest reports confirm they are digging up *diamonds*!

'The minister of foreign relations found an old parchment outlining an agreement between our two kingdoms. It dates from your father's time,' he told Ajatashatru, 'and it says that the mine shall be shared equally. But for one reason or another, our side has not enforced this. And since this mine is on the opposite bank, *all the labour* has been provided by the Licchavis, and the Licchavis have been carting away *all of the gems*.'

'Their chiefs sure are getting fat,' muttered Ajatashatru. He raised a questioning eyebrow. 'It is within the borders of Pattanagama after all. Can we not lay fair claim to it?'

Vassakaara scratched at his beard. 'It doesn't look good for us. You father had close ties with the Licchavis. Not to mention, they are your mother's family.'

Ajatashatru waved his arm dismissively.

'Even setting that aside,' the minister persisted, 'Vaishali isn't a pushover. They are strong in their allies, wealthy enough to bear a long war and hold a well-trained...'

A commotion at the door caused both men to cease their talk and look up.

'My lady, my lady! You *really* cannot go in now!'

'Step aside, I say! How dare a sentry bar me from seeing my husband.'

'Ho! Step aside there!' commanded Ajatashatru.

The guards lowered their spears and an enraged beauty sailed into the room. Her flashing eyes took in the fact that the king was not alone and she stopped abruptly. Vassakaara stepped off the dais and bowed to her. Padmavati bit her lips and stood pouting as if reconsidering her words before the royal adviser.

Ajatashatru came forward, took both her hands into his own and said indulgently, 'What good fortune to see you so early in the day, my dear.'

Padmavati peeked beyond him to ensure the minister was not eavesdropping, then whispered petulantly to the king, 'Would that my morning had been as good.'

'Oh? And who dared upset my spitfire?' questioned the bemused king.

Padmavati's eyes flashed and she withdrew her hands.

'It pleases you to make light of me now. But when you hear what I have to say, will you still be so pleased, I wonder!'

'Come, come,' replied the king, taking her hands again. 'Sit down and tell us the whole.'

Padmavati allowed herself to be drawn to a seat. Inhaling with exaggerated patience, she said, 'I was eating sweets on the balcony some days back when who should pass by in the garden below but your brothers Halla and Vihalla. They were atop Sechanaka – you remember the great white elephant that the late king, your father, fought and tamed? Their wives were also with them. All seated in a large, jewelled howdah.

'As I looked on, I saw that one of them wore the eighteen-fold string of divine pearls, which too came from Father-in-law, for I well remember when it was first presented in court. How wondrous was the luminescence of each exquisite bead.

'Now that I see them again, it seems that such extraordinary treasures – both the elephant and the pearls – should not be in the hands of mere princes. They ought to belong to the king, just as they did in your father's time.'

Ajatashatru patted her hands and replied, 'My dear, he bequeathed those items to my brothers, just as he bequeathed to me his entire kingdom. Call for merchants if you wish and pick what treasures you like. Why bother with what Halla and Vihalla have.'

Padmavati replied, 'Even the maids passing by the garden say it is not the king who enjoys the real treasures of the kingdom but these two *kumaras*, Halla and Vihalla. I knew you could not be bothered, sire. But it is no matter. I have already sent word to them that a gift of these treasures would please us greatly.'

She smiled impishly up at him through her lashes. Her audacity pleased Ajatashatru. He liked his queen to throw her weight around and compel others to fulfil her whims and demands.

'And so you are now the new owner of the great white Sechanaka and the fabled eighteen-string pearls,' he assessed. 'What then has you in a temper?'

'Oh! That's just it – I am not the owner. Those cowardly princes! They claimed the treasures were theirs and refused to part with them. Rather than doing so, they chose to leave the palace! As soon as I heard, I sent an order to bring them back. Is our arm so powerless or our royal reach so short? But this morning I hear, they've fled the capital!'

Ajatashatru frowned. The treasures were one thing. Flouting royal authority was another matter entirely. It set a dangerous precedent to let princes of the blood get away with disobedience. He signalled to Vassakaara.

'Guards!' commanded the minister and two sturdy warriors materialized in the room. 'Despatch a force immediately and invite the princes Halla and Vihalla to attend their king.'

The men saluted and left.

That evening, while Ajatashatru and Vassakaara continued to ponder the question of how best to acquire the mines of Pattanagama, news came to them about Halla and Vihalla. The soldiers had chased the recalcitrant duo to the very banks of the Ganga. But once they slipped across that border into Vaishali, there was little to be done. Through official channels, they discovered that Halla and Vihalla had taken refuge with their formidable maternal grandfather Chetaka, a chief of Vaishali.

As he heard this, a gleam appeared in Ajatashatru's eyes. He looked over at his minister and caught sight of Vassakaara's smirk. The same idea had struck them both: they now had a reason to fight Vaishali! A lawful reason. No one could say they were warring against family for profit... no, they were simply fighting to liberate their brothers from the clutches of a neighbouring state, one that had secretly deprived them of their rightful wealth at that!

As confident as they were, they proceeded with care. Ajatashatru pretended to reason using diplomatic channels. Three times he sent word to Chetaka, demanding that his brothers be sent back to him, and three times he was rejected.

Gleefully, the king prepared for war. 'I will exterminate them, however powerful and mighty they may be.'

Still, Vassakaara cautioned him.

'The Licchavis are no meek clan that will bow to our threats. Chetaka alone could decimate our soldiers. He holds back only for being a disciplined, practising Jain. With him being so noble, so grey with long leadership, many high-minded rulers of other states feel compelled to follow his command. They will be pleased too, to join a war against us and carve up our territories among themselves.'

Through such counsel, Ajatashatru came to believe that an outright war with Vaishali could not guarantee him success.

'If the brute strength of my army will not lead us to victory,' he said, 'there must still be other ways to overcome the Licchavis. Vassakaara, we hear that the Enlightened One is now at Vulture's Peak. Seek him out and share our intentions with him. Paint him a picture of this coming war in the clearest, bloodiest terms and let him know that should he wish to save lives, he must

direct us towards a better way. No one in the world is wiser than him. One way or another, his words will aid us.

'Bear my words in mind, Vassakaara, and repeat them exactly as I say them to you. Be careful too that you remember the Great One's words – his manner, his expression – so you may bring back a true account of his reply.'

Thus it was that the minister found himself at Vulture's Peak, exchanging courtesies with the monks of the *sangha*.

The Buddha sat at his shaded station and Ananda, his disciple, fanned him gently against the great heat of the day.

'Revered Gautama,' said Vassakaara, 'King Ajatashatru of Magadha, the son of Queen Vaidehi, pays homage at your feet. He enquires after your health, whether you are free from affliction and disease, whether you are well, fit and at ease. Venerable sir, the king wishes to make war against the Licchavi princes of Vaishali. He is making glorious declarations of exterminating the chiefs, however powerful and mighty they may be, and that he will set the demons of chaos among them and cause their ruin.'

The Buddha smiled. He asked his disciple, 'Ananda, do the rulers of Licchavi hold meetings frequently? Do they meet many times? What have you heard?'

Ananda replied, 'Venerable sir, I have heard that the republic's rulers hold meetings frequently. Indeed, none of them ever skips a meeting once it's scheduled.'

The Buddha nodded in approval. 'The advantage of frequent meetings is that fresh information is always forthcoming from all directions. Unrest at remote places and border areas will not then go unnoticed; no breach of law and order will go unreported. So long as the princes assemble regularly and share their information, they are bound to prosper; there is no reason for their decline.

'Ananda,' he continued, 'do the Vaishali rulers assemble and disperse in harmony? Do they act harmoniously to discharge their duties on behalf of their country?'

'Venerable One, it is as you say. The princes are in harmony from beginning to end, and every action is taken in the care of their nation. They shoulder their responsibilities equally.'

'If that is so,' replied the Buddha, 'then no space will be given for suspicion or ill will to take root. They are bound to prosper; there is no reason for their decline. Ananda, do they follow time-honoured traditions and practices? Do they treat their fellows with courtesy? Do they respect the wisdom of elders? Do they protect those who are innocent, vulnerable and needy? What have you heard?'

'Venerable sir, all these practices they hold in high regard. They heed good advice, uphold the rights of those who need protection, they give a voice to the voiceless, they value gratitude and prayer, and they practise charity.'

'Ananda, so long as the rulers of Vaishali value these practices, people will thrive on their lands. In such genial atmosphere, the princes are also bound to prosper; there is no reason for their decline.'

Then the Buddha said to Vassakaara, 'Brahmin, these are the principles that I taught Vaishali when I stayed at the Saarandada shrine. So long as these factors of growth remain with them, so long as they abide by them, Vaishali is bound to prosper; there is no reason for its decline.'

Vassakaara replied, 'Revered Gautama, just abiding by any one of these factors of growth could ensure prosperity. How much more so would Vaishali prosper if they carefully abide by all of them! O Blessed One, it is not likely that my king will conquer Vaishali simply by making war upon it. Revered Gautama, I shall take leave now. There are many affairs to attend to.'

Vassakaara returned brooding to the palace, busy turning over the implications of the Buddha's words. His wily brain hatched a plan and he hurried to share it with his master.

Not long after, Ajatashatru raised the matter of conquering Vaishali at court before all his advisers and commanders. He made his royal will clear. Yet, Vassakaara dared to raise his voice against it.

'The wise seer had clearly stated how damaging it would be to attack our neighbour. Why then should we risk the loss of life and resources in a futile war?'

The disagreement between the two escalated into stubborn words and ever-fiercer accusations. That day, the court dispersed and went home in small groups and tense whispers.

The next day, when the court reconvened, Vassakaara was brought in chains in front of the king. The courtiers were astonished. The arresting officer read out the charges against him: Vassakaara had been caught sending gifts to the Vaishali princes. The presents, seized at the border by vigilant officials, were displayed as evidence.

Surely this was the end of the minister, many thought, not daring to look at their king's face as it turned increasingly purple with rage. Yet, Ajatashatru did not explode. Instead, he considered Vassakaara's long, faithful record and gave him a proper trial. The matter was thoroughly investigated, but its outcome remained the same – the minister was condemned as a traitor.

Still, the king was lenient. In view of his long years of service to the court of Magadha, Vassakaara was spared execution and instead exiled from the kingdom. As many expected, he went over to Vaishali. The city received him with mixed feelings.

Vaishali elected a circle of rulers from its more influential families. Some of these noblemen felt that a minister once so close to the ferocious Ajatashatru must be a keeper of many vital state secrets. What good luck to obtain such a valuable knight in their game of chess! Should Ajatashatru move against them, no doubt Vassakaara could check the opponent.

Yet others advised caution against a man so crooked, a man who had betrayed his country and changed loyalties so lightly. Let him not cross the Ganga, they said. Who would show kindness to a viper and expect benefits in return?

In the end, the Licchavis took pity on Vassakaara. They allowed him some space in their city to stay and teach for a living. And since many among the ruling families admired the Brahmin for his exceptional learning, they soon began to study the princely arts from him. Eventually, Vassakaara proved so valuable, so indispensable, that many began to vie for his attention. Each wanted to be the favoured student of this guru.

'What were you talking to him about?' a Licchavi prince would ask another, who had spent some private time with the minister.

'Nothing much, just about what I had for breakfast today.'

What a queer thing for a learned minister to talk about, the first prince would think. *There is surely more to this that he's not telling me.*

Other princes also held meetings with the minister. But when their fellows enquired, the answer was always so very inconsequential – we talked of oxen, or we talked of the latest fashions – that soon a sense of distrust drove a wedge between the men.

Matters began to escalate.

Vassakaara once said to a prince in private, 'Your Highness, it pains me to be the bearer of this news, but it is best you know: someone has been spreading rumours that you are a coward.'

'Who dares call me a coward?' asked the amazed prince.

'Oh, it was that prince Ra— who did so.'

Thus, enmity arose between two princes of Licchavi.

Little by little, using seemingly inconsequential actions, poisonous whispers and a web of hearsay, Vassakaara broke the unity of the ruling body. After three years, he decided to test the success of his scheme. He sent out a town crier to beat a gong and call the princes to assemble.

Driven apart by suspicion and resentment, each prince sulked and refused to go. *If I am such a coward, if I am so untrustworthy, let the brave, noble ones go to the assembly! Why should they bother with me. Why should I bother with them!*

Thoughts such as these held them back. When the time came to gather, no one turned up.

Vassakaara was delighted. Now the princes were no longer following the Buddha's advice. He despatched a secret courier to Ajatashatru.

Master, said his missive, *your scheme – carefully planted and cultivated by this ever-faithful yeoman – has at last borne fruit. Should it please you, the time to harvest is now.*

In three years, Ajatashatru had made his own preparations for war. Pattanagama was fortified heavily for defence and quick strikes against the enemy. While Vaishali's men undercut each other, Magadha's soldiers developed new, advanced forms of warfare. Magadhan engineers invented weapons like giant catapults and a terrifying new chariot to cause maximum damage to the enemy's forces – from afar and at close quarters!

On receiving Vassakaara's message, Ajatashatru called his men to arms. There came to him ten half-brothers, each leading three thousand horses, three thousand elephants, three thousand chariots and thirty thousand infantrymen. With this almighty host behind him, the king declared war on Vaishali.

The Licchavi faction had long since ceased to listen to its intelligence reports. The sudden appearance of an enemy at the gates set them panicking. Nine leaders of the Mallas, nine Licchavi chiefs and eighteen kings of Kasi–Kosala answered grand old Chetaka's call to rally. But the princes were no longer united in thought, word or deed.

'We will not let them cross the Gaṅga!' they each said, but when an assembly was ordered to discuss the resistance, each still nursed old grudges. 'Let the brave ones go!' they declared in derision. And no one attended.

When Ajatashatru's forces crossed the Ganga, the princes of Vaishali proclaimed, 'We will not let them enter our city. We will close our city gates and stand firm. Come! To our defences now!'

They shouted and tried to convene a council. Yet, there was no unanimous response.

When the armies finally clashed, Chetaka fought mightily, bringing down each of Ajatashatru's half-brothers over ten days of hard battle. Yet, in the end, the disunity of the Licchavis left their army as disarrayed as grains of rice on a plate. And their astute enemy scooped them up and polished them off easily.

In the ensuing mayhem, Sechanaka, the noble white elephant, fell into a pit dug by Ajatashatru's soldiers. There it breathed its last, impaled by iron rods and burned by hot coals. Not long after, Chetaka, a devout Jain, chose to practise *sallekahna* (a ritual fast unto death). Halla and Vihalla became monks under the holy order of Mahavira. The gates to Vaishali stood wide open. Ajatashatru's armies flooded through, massacred the remaining princes and returned to Rajagriha in complete victory.

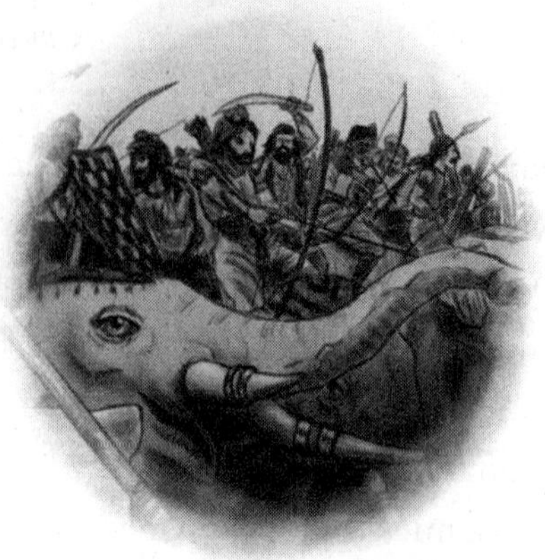

THE INDOMITABLE GAUR

These were the dying days of the Gupta dynasty, when the once mighty house had become a shadow of its former self. Its western regions had been ravaged by Hun armies. Its great centres of learning and valuable trade routes lay in ruins. Its rulers had become feeble and power had shifted into the hands of its ministers.

In the chaos of the collapsing empire, adventuring warriors and politicians seized the chance to carve out their own territories and establish their own royal courts. New lords emerged in the neighbouring Deccan regions and proved stronger than the Guptas. Kingdoms rose, clashed and fell with the fate of their leaders. During these turbulent days, a wily minister staked his claim in the east. He named his new lands Gauda and he, Shashanka, was eager to expand his territory and become king.

•-•-•-•-•-•-•-•-•-•

Under a pearl-white sky, the wreckage of a recent battle ripened under the hot sun. On the broad pasture where men had roared and elephants rampaged just hours earlier, there was now only the silence of victorious pennants whipped by the winds and the occasional screech of scavengers.

Shashanka of Gauda rested on a makeshift platform among his advisers and generals. Couriers lined up to deliver reports, some from the battlefield and some from the capital far away. The king fired back his orders and the messengers scampered away down the channel.

'Without the elephant force this time,' Shashanka assessed, 'we would have lost more men, and possibly years, in conquering Kamarupa.'

'Here is a runner with more good news,' cried out a minister on the far left, 'from Kannauj.'

'What does he say?' asked the Gaur. 'Have our allies liberated the city?'

'Just as you foresaw, sire. What a glorious victory added to this one today. To craft a winning strategy over so strong a foe as the Maukhri while you are miles away – this will go down in song.'

'Ha! Strong they may have been, but they were upstarts nevertheless. How could they expect to be command the loyalty of so ancient and vast a territory as Magadha from Kannauj. They would have done better to make allies with their neighbours as Bimbisara did in the old days. As it is, we only spread a few stories questioning the legitimacy of their rule, and all the princes flocked to our banner and rose against them!'

'But what shall we do with the many princes now, sire? They have settled at Kannauj and are waiting to portion the land among themselves.'

'They couldn't go up against the Maukhris on their own. But they dare to take me on – me, who defeated that powerful dynasty? We shall see. What is the situation in the city?'

'When the allied army breached the palace, they killed King Grihavarma and imprisoned Queen Rajyashri. Since then, many of the princes have banded under the leadership of the ruler of Malwa. They are clamouring for a share of the spoils. Malwa – who hates the Maukhris with a vengeance – is even demanding that he be given the deposed queen!'

Shashanka stroked his beard and spoke, 'We already knew Devagupta of Malwa would ask for her. His purpose was glaringly obvious when he allied with us. This lady… is she not the daughter of the old Vardhan ruler at Sthaneshwar?'

'Indeed, sire,' replied another adviser. 'Only, that old one has gone to meet his Maker. His eldest son, Rajyavardhan, now holds the throne.'

'Give her to our friend Devagupta.'

The advisers snuck unhappy looks at each other. The family at Sthaneshwar was just as powerful as the Maukhris had been. There were far better ways of dealing with a daughter of that house than handing her over to her family's sworn enemy.

Shashanka cut through his ministers' awkward grumbling. He gripped the nearest one by his forearm and spoke firmly.

'Send her to Malwa, I said!' Then he added, 'But send also a messenger to her brother Rajyavardhan. Extend our goodwill to him, describe our admiration of his person and say that we wish to become his friend. As proof of this friendship, tell him that we have news of his sister – that Devagupta of Malwa has murdered her husband and kidnapped her!'

'But Malwa is our friend, sire. Do we throw him away like this?'

'Did you not say that Malwa has banded with other princes behind our back? Should we allow them to steal Kannauj from us and still call him a friend? Humph! Be sure to send the lady to Malwa and send him back to his kingdom. He must be well gone before Rajyavardhan hears our news.'

'And what of the other princes?' asked another adviser.

'Remove the leader and the rest will fall apart. Once Malwa is gone, they will not know how to press their case. While they run about like headless chickens, despatch their forces outside the city under the pretence of keeping peace in the nearby areas. As their troops leave the gates, bring more of ours into Kannauj to maintain order *within* the city. Over this month, we must ensure that the walls enclose more of our soldiers than theirs.'

He turned over the stratagem in his mind, looking for weak spots.

'Tell our spies,' he added, 'to sow discord among the princes. We must not have any other take lead... one Malwa is enough!'

He looked about the great battalions standing in the field and grinned, 'Now we are needed here no more. Let us take this army to Kannauj as well. We shall see what our *allies* have to say.'

'We have one last duty to attend here, sire,' reminded the minister. He raised his arm and beckoned to a cohort of guards nearby. They came forward, escorting two men in chains.

The older of the two strode up to the platform, bent his knee before Shashanka and said, 'I, Supratishta, have this day lost Kamarupa on the battlefield. I have lost the right to call myself king. Accept the throne, noble Shashanka. If you hold anger from this war, may it fall solely upon my head. And may you treat your new subjects kindly as their true sovereign.'

Shashanka's pleased gaze lingered upon the bowed figure. Then he gave a leisurely signal. The minister of war sprang up from his seat, descended the platform in manufactured haste and raised Supratishta to his feet.

'Royal One, rise quickly,' he said, 'our lord has no desire to take your throne away.'

Supratishta took a surprised step backwards, but the minister held him fast.

'So long as you pay tribute to the mighty Gaur of Bengal and accept him as your liege, Kamarupa will remain in your hands.'

Supratishta fell to both knees this time and vowed fealty to Shashanka in a shaking voice. Behind him, his brother Bhaskara glowered. Supratishta caught sight of it and pulled the young man down. At his command, Bhaskara grovelled before the platform and mumbled words of loyalty.

Still, his proud heart burned with anger and resentment. He remembered how his father had been killed by the Gauda army. How their retreating soldiers had been torn apart by rampaging battle elephants. He turned his head aside, unable to see his noble brother genuflecting to a mere minister of the Guptas. Allegiance, hah! How could he vow so, when resentments beyond count dug into his guts. Rancour churned and drew bile in his throat. A plan for vengeance began to take shape. He was glad to have overheard the Gaur's plot against Malwa and Rajyavardhan.

Harsha wrestled with nightmares even as the sky lightened, summoning dawn. As the rays fell upon his smooth young cheek, his eyes opened. The feverish haze gradually dissipated and the boy-king sat up.

No nightmare could surpass the real ordeals of his recent days.

Backed by a ten-thousand-strong army, his brother Rajyavardhan had marched to Malwa and defeated the cur who had abducted their sister. But no clue of Rajyashri had been found in the city.

More mysteriously still, Rajyavardhan had gone to meet his friend Shashanka and lost his life soon after. Harsha, whose voice had broken not a year ago, was now the last of his direct line. The court crowned him hastily and he set about gathering an army.

Who else but the Gaur could be responsible, he thought in the flurry of activity. One so great as his brother would not be easy to harm, let alone kill. The Gaur must have got past his defences under the pretence of friendship. *Oh brother, did you see it coming? How vilely you must have felt the betrayal! And what of Sister? Is Rajyashri too hidden away somewhere by that miscreant?*

Harsha proclaimed war and eager warriors rallied to his banner. Men who held a grudge against Shashanka – for his tactics made him as many enemies as allies – gathered at Sthaneshwar. Men who sought to make a name for themselves in those troubled days also flocked to the stern new king. Not least were the vassals of the house of Vardhan, made strong under the rule of his father and brother.

Harshavardhan set out with an army so large and fierce that it made his neighbours uneasy. Yet, they dared not impede his progress through their lands. Indeed, more fighters flocked to his standard as the force wound smoothly and with deadly purpose to its destination.

Prince Bhaskara of Kamarupa was one of these who joined on the way. He sent his messenger to extend a hand to the rising power.

'Long and glorious be your rule, sire,' said the man, bowing before Harsha's warhorse. 'I am Hansbeg, and I come bearing gifts and warm words of friendship from Prince Bhaskara of Kamarupa. If it be your purpose to bring down the Gaur of Bengal, the prince willingly swears his armies and himself to your cause.' Thus, Harsha's support swelled like a river in monsoon.

On another arduous day of marching, Harsha was stopped by the sudden arrival of his cousin and staunch adviser Bhandi. The minister's expressions fluctuated between joy and concern as he addressed the king.

'Sire, at last we have news of the princess.'

Harsha vaulted off his horse, strode towards Bhandi and gripped him by the shoulders. 'Is she well? Is she here? Speak up, man!' he commanded.

'She is alive,' Bhandi reassured him. 'As to the rest, it is hard to say. For certain she has escaped her bonds. But she did not then look for her brothers, her cousins or any who could have helped her return home.

The last sight of her was near the wilderness of the Vindhyachal mountains.'

Harsha trembled to hear this. *If his sister was free, why had she not come home? He stared at the formidable forested peaks before him. Why would a queen, delicately raised, brave such a terrible jungle? How long before she injured herself, starved or fell prey to the wild animals of the Vindhyas?*

'Bhandi, I must look for her while there is still a chance. Until I find her, take my place and lead this army. I will join you soon, God willing.'

So saying, Harsha selected a handful of men to follow him and swooped down upon the forests, searching for his sister. The chiefs of the lands came out to offer him help. By passing the word around and by soliciting the aid of locals, they combed the jungle section by section.

In this rigorous search of the tricky terrain, Harsha's group stumbled across a woman who was raking together bits of wood and dead leaves into a long pile. Her thin calloused hands, bleeding feet, muddied torn robes and ragged hair all spoke of extreme suffering.

Harsha approached her and asked, 'Sister, would you raise your face and speak with me?'

When the lady pushed her hair back and looked up, Harsha recognized the familiar, now grief-stricken, features of his beloved sibling. His eyes filled with tears and he gathered her close, praising God he had found her in time.

Rajyashri stroked his head and said, 'I am glad I was able to see you one last time before I join my husband in the afterlife.'

Harsha now understood that the pile she was creating was meant to be a pyre. Rajyashri's great trials had left her severely depressed, but Harsha would not allow her to take her life. Alternately commanding and coaxing her, he and his men convinced her to give up the foolish idea. They promised Rajyashri that her wrongs would be paid back tenfold to Shashanka. With this hope, the princess finally agreed to return with them.

His sister's safety seen to, Harsha resumed his trek towards Kannauj. With Devagupta's death, the loss of his allies and Bhandi's enormous army at the gate, Shashanka strategically retreated to Gauda. The throne of Kannauj thus fell to Harsha by universal acclaim. Impressed with its wealth and its strategic position in the empire, Harsha moved his capital from Sthaneshwar to Kannauj.

From there, he launched an attack on Magadha, which Shashanka had wrested from the Maukhris. But before the army could go on the offensive, the ruler of Magadha surrendered and sued for peace. Harsha's empire was on the rise.

Not forgetting his promise to his sister, he attacked Gauda. He attacked many times over several years. Each time, he was repulsed by stratagem and strength. With passing time, Harsha became so mighty that the powerful Tang emperor of China sent ambassadors to his court. Nevertheless, Shashanka remained an aggressive threat as long as he lived.

It wasn't until Shashanka's son, the less capable Manava, came to the throne that Harsha was able to settle matters with that clan. In the days following Shashanka's death, Bhaskara and Harsha conquered Gauda and divided it up – but they could not extinguish the Gaur's name. The later kings of Bengal venerated Shashanka as their first king and drew their titles from his as Gaureshwar – lords of Gauda.

THE TROUBLE WITH TWIN KINGS

Hiranya let his head fall back against the soft rugs as his attendant massaged the aching knots in his calves. His storyteller, standing by the glowing hearth, half sang, half narrated the tales of a hero long gone. Outside, winds bellowed around the fort and thunder crashed through the darkening sky.

All of a sudden, Hiranya felt a rush of joy thrill through his tired body. It was as welcome as it was unexpected, and he smiled. Somewhere, something good had just happened to Toramana. It must be extraordinarily good, for his brother to feel such delight.

In a few moments, the fort buzzed with new activity, though the stormy night was settling deeper upon it. Lamps were relit, and threw long shadows down the stony corridors. Cheers and laughter ebbed and flowed outside Hiranya's chamber. He was about to inquire after the hubbub when a messenger demanded entrance.

'Sire,' he said, reaching Hiranya's feet in breathless excitement, 'you are to be heartily congratulated! The physician has been to see your sister-in-law, Queen Anjana. This humble servant rejoices to say, the lady is with child! The king is with child! The kingdom will have an heir!'

The world dimmed before Hiranya's eyes. The noise receded. In the rising blackness, Hiranya could see the day, fourteen years before, when he and his twin held their weddings. The cacophony of celebrations matched and melded. He could see their father as he pressed the royal astrologers to look into the siblings' future.

'Toramana's union will be blessed with a child, a son, who will be heir to the house,' the greybeards foretold.

'And what of Hiranya?' their father asked.

The astrologers looked uncomfortably at their feet and said nothing.

Hiranya accepted the heavy silence for it meant nothing to him. Prophecies were often wrong. And even if this one came true, what did it matter? Toramana's child would be as welcome, as beloved as a child of his own. The twins were of one mind and heart, even if their bodies were separate. Indeed, when Toramana was sick, so was Hiranya. When Hiranya broke his leg, Toramana fainted from the pain. Between two such bonded souls, what did it matter who sired the future heir?

So now, when the child was a reality, why was Hiranya filled with this inexplicable, burning emotion? He didn't even know what he felt, only that it moved him to violence. He spat out vile curses. Toramana could not have a son, at least not before him. Hiranya was older, even if only by two minutes. The first child must be his own!

The celebrations eventually died down. The revellers drew each other into smaller parties and drifted away. In one wing of the fort, Toramana and Anjana remained too joyous to fall asleep. They lay talking and planning in whispers, ignoring the echoes of thunder that hammered at their walls.

They could not, however, ignore the sudden rapping of a heavy wooden stick.

Even as Toramana picked up a lamp and moved to the entrance, the knocking grew louder and more insistent. Throwing open the doors, he found the old court astrologer outside.

'Lord, forgive this haste, but we have little time! Your brother is sending men to arrest you both. We must leave. Now!'

Toramana stared at him, speechless. What possessed this old fogey to come so late to his door, and with such a tale! The man had lost his wits!

Anjana too heard the astrologer. Coming up from behind her husband, she spoke soothingly, 'Reverend sir, calm yourself. What has upset you?'

Impatiently, the elder scolded them, 'Many years ago, my lord and lady will recall, we prophesied the birth of your son. We had hoped that with clear knowledge beforehand, your brother would make peace with his destiny. All these years, you have ruled together and never has he shown the slightest animosity, not by look or word. Yet, we watched him closely for the sake of the kingdom – and a good thing we did! This news has been a blow to him, and he is sending men this way to try and change fate.

'For the safety of this precious child, for securing our kingdom's future, you must come away now, sire. Speedily, I beg you both!'

Toramana refused. Hiranya, his own blood twin, the companion of his childhood mischiefs and now his co-ruler – how could he turn against them for such a reason? It was impossible. His disbelief took another turn.

'Have you set your men to spy on your own king?!' he demanded.

The astrologer took a deep breath and put forth his case once more. His urgency was sincere, and Anjana, with newfound motherly instinct, claimed she would rather be safe than sorry. Toramana, still displeased and disbelieving, refused to leave but allowed Anjana to be taken away. Her most faithful maids and a guard of proven men were despatched to keep them safe.

This will all prove a misunderstanding, he thought, *and I will have her back soon.*

He was still sceptical when guards showed up and escorted him to Hiranya's wing. As he entered his brother's chambers, Toramana took in the mess – the torn tapestries, smashed vessels and scrolls in disarray – and grew uneasy.

'Brother, what do you require of me so late at night?' he demanded.

Hiranya lounged on his rugs, brooding over a sword. 'Ah. The hour is indeed late. Though your messenger just relayed the news of your little joy, I am already late in offering felicitations. Our fort has been ringing with revelry and *I am late* in joining the celebrations. So, I invite our little family to bring in the cheer. I did not ask you alone… where is my gentle sister-in-law?'

'She is not here.'

'*Where is she?*' asked Hiranya, eyes closed.

'I did not wish to disturb her and left her behind.'

A messenger came in and bowed before the twin kings.

'Speak,' directed Hiranya.

'The lady has left the fort, sire. There is no sign of her.'

Toramana grew angry. 'Why are you searching for my wife in this manner?'

'I wish to make you two comfortable until my nephew is born.'

Toramana's gaze narrowed. 'This cannot be! I did not believe it when they told me. Yet, here you are, hunting down my family – *your own* family! – in the middle of the night. I see it now. I *feel* it, Hiranya. This scorching black rage. It comes from you, does it not? Tell me why!'

Hiranya stayed silent. Toramana's despair twisted his guts into knots, but other more powerful emotions made him ignore the pain.

Toramana tried again. 'Do you remember the day we were crowned? The court stood in a circle – intense and silent – around us. Not one of them could tell us apart, though they'd seen us our whole lives. We faced the empty throne and swore before the ministers and the priests to be true and united to our father's will. Do you remember Father's will?'

Hiranya swallowed and clenched the rug.

'Noblemen, wise advisers and brave guardians of our state, all stood witness to it,' Toramana reminded him. 'Father feared that troublemakers would sow dissent after his passing. That is why he left a royal edict, so no one would question his final word. He praised *both of us* for showing wisdom before scholars, valour before warriors and humility before teachers. He commended both of us for excelling in logic and diplomacy, for being strong in ambition and clear in vision. And as we are thus equal by birth and equally capable in form, will and execution, he bade that we jointly rule, taking the throne by turn. Two heads, he said, would be wiser than one.

'Not one man stood against his decision. They cheered: *Long live King Hiranya! Long live King Toramana!* Do you remember all this, brother? He left an edict for *them*! Because he never once dreamed that you and I would fight each other!'

Hiranya stood up. 'I will not harm you or your wife,' he said at last.

'Ha!' spat Toramana. 'You have no right. We are equal! Both of us dress in royal robes. Both of us took part in the *abhishekam* and were anointed co-rulers. There are as many coins minted with my face as with yours. The administration needs my stamp as much as yours. The army follows my tally as does it yours!'

'Yet, I rule first!' shouted Hiranya. 'I was born first. And I took the throne that first year while you advised at my side.'

'And now you are the first to seek an end to us! Will you kill my son, your own flesh and blood? No! Before that I will end us both!'

So saying, Toramana ran full tilt at one of the guards. Instinctively, the man angled his spear and it pierced Toramana's side. Hiranya bellowed as he felt his brother's pain slice through him. The guard hastily pulled back and Toramana crumpled, bleeding, to the floor. In one fluid motion, Hiranya wrenched the spear from the erring hand and rammed it straight into the guard's chest.

'My son will become the ruler as prophesied and you will die with me!' hissed Toramana as he lost consciousness.

Hiranya was crippled with pain. 'Fetch the physician,' he gasped, as darkness overtook him.

When he came to, Hiranya's body was in an agony of fever. The physician at his side warned him, 'Sire, something must be done about your brother. He rips his bandages, tears at his flesh and is thrashing about in a deathly delirium. When he harms himself, he harms you.'

Hiranya took great draughts of the opiate that was handed to him. He then rose and dragged his shaking frame to Toramana's side.

'Look, you!' he grasped his brother's hands and cried into his agitated eyes. 'I have sent hundreds of soldiers after Anjana. They will seek her out and when they find her…'

Toramana's thrashing stilled upon those words. He stared unfocused at the ceiling, his every nerve straining to hear what Hiranya would say next.

'Where can one gentle noblewoman hide in such a short time? I will find her and rip the child from out of her belly! BUT!' he cried as Toramana keened into a fit again.

'But, if you agree to stay alive, move far from the capital and live by my rules, I will call the men back. I will cease all attempts to find her. What do you say?'

Toramana shut his eyes. Tears seeped out as he considered the choices. Then he nodded his acquiescence.

In a matter of days, Toramana publicly resigned from his duties, stating ill health. Far from the capital, a cave was prepared for him. Here, he was kept masked and closely guarded, so none could know the identity of the prisoner. They only knew he was noble, for he was surrounded by comforts and could have almost anything for the asking. He was given good food, his health was scrupulously monitored and no harm, however small, was allowed to befall him. Yet, he was strictly isolated and none dared speak with him for fear that their heads would roll.

Fourteen years thus passed by. Toramana lived in his cage, sustained by the hope of being reunited with his wife and child someday. In his possession were a handful of coins that bore his stamp. He would look upon them and yearn for the days gone by. With only nostalgia and regret for company, his hopes begin to dwindle year by year, and with it, his will to stay alive. Every day, he ate more sparingly and became more listless.

Hiranya could not help but notice. His body reflected the changes. The doctor could find no reason for his decline.

A king cannot afford to be seen as weakening: not in his decisions, not in his relations with family or subjects, not even in sport. And yet Hiranya watched others watch him get weaker. When he could bear it no longer, he visited his brother and chastised Toramana for putting their kingdom at risk.

Receiving no response, the enraged ruler ripped the visor off the prisoner's face. A living mask, skeletal and grey, greeted him. Hiranya stumbled back. It was like his own face in death's grip.

Seized by a new sense of urgency, he took his brother by the shoulders and shook him.

'You must live, do you hear me! If our life does not matter to you,' he fumed, 'live for your family! Remember our pact. So long as you stay whole and healthy, Anjana is safe from me. But I tell you now, if you do not improve, I will seek out your wife and child and see them die before you can end me!'

Toramana jerked backed to his senses. It was as if great veils of cobwebs had shrouded his mind over the years. Hiranya's threats blew them away in one trumpeting blast.

My wife and son, he thought. *I will never see them again unless I do something about it myself!*

To his brother he said, 'I will try.'

Hiranya rose, frustrated, and stormed out of the prison. He did not notice that, behind him, his brother's long-term jailer stood stock-still in shock. He had seen the resemblance between the king and the unmasked captive.

The jailer stood rooted and unsure. The prisoner was not chatty. And it was no doubt best to stay out of the king's business. He was startled, therefore, when pity and curiosity fuelled his walk back to Toramana's small room. With a sigh of resignation, he unlocked the door and greeted the man within.

'Is all well with you, sir?' he asked respectfully.

A newly revived Toramana seized the chance. He answered not directly, but said, 'When the king himself looks in on me and cares for my well-being, what complaints can there be?'

'It is good of you to say so,' replied the jailer, 'but you are visited by none other. For all the comforts you are allowed, you must still be lonely. If you wish to unburden yourself, this inconsequential man before you would willingly hear your complaints… and do his humble best to ease your woes.'

At this simple urging, Toramana felt the dam of his sorrows break and the tale poured out of him. Such a flood of passion, long held in check, came gushing forth that the jailer was swept away in the force. Toramana narrated stories small and big, of brothers growing up, of love and family, of corrupting powers and betrayals. It took days, and the jailer hung on to every word even as he was rocked by the storm of emotions.

When his story drew to a close, the jailer departed. He did not lock the access behind him. Warily, Toramana tried it and the door gave way. He tiptoed down the long tunnel, but it seemed unnecessary – the guards were not at their posts. He reached the mouth of the cave and found that the gates of his prison stood wide open.

He took a step on to the road. The sun shone brightly. Toramana, pale and emaciated from long incarceration, winced and huddled back into the cool shade. As his skin and eyes adjusted to daylight, he saw a cart drawing up the road. He shrank back into a crevice of a roadside rock, afraid of being discovered.

He need not have worried. The bullock cart drew up to the prison gates and the jailer sprang down from the driver's seat. He gathered up a set of clothes and approached Toramana.

'Forgive this humble carriage, sire,' he said, 'but it will be strong enough to carry you back to the capital.'

He held out the robes. Toramana wrapped the cloak over his head and followed the jailer back to the cart. Food had been prepared for him and a comfortable seat laid out. The jailer held out the bullock's reins and bowed to Toramana.

Long had it been since Toramana had stood in the light, since someone had called him 'sire' or shown loyalty to his cause. He breathed in deeply, as if it were his first taste of air. Then he reached into his worn-out underclothes and brought forth a handful of old coins.

Handing them to the jailer, he said, 'Good friend, these coins were minted when I first took the throne. They may seem like your king's coins, but notice how the face looks the other way. Those who are faithful to me will also know what coins these are.

'When I leave here, I must find my son and make him king as was prophesied. The prince will need supporters. Will you gather those who remain loyal to me and wait for my word?'

The jailer bowed, 'For a long time after you disappeared, sire, a multitude of soldiers, merchants, scholars and noblemen raised a storm, demanding to see you. They clamoured to know why you resigned so suddenly and where you were residing. They must be waiting for your return still. I will seek them and rebuild ties so that when it is time for the prince to raise his banner, he will have support in money, minds and arms.'

A frail but buoyed Toramana thus set out for the capital.

The sun was just setting when Jayendra, Anjana's brother, returned home. Close by his doorstep, a starved, tattered beggar extended his bowl.

'You, there!' Jayendra called to his sentry. 'Send someone from the kitchen with food and clothes for this poor man.'

As the guard left to do as asked, Jayendra felt the beggar clutch his ankle. In surprise he looked down, and found himself staring into familiar eyes.

'You!' cried Jayendra, nearly keeling over in shock.

In a flash, he took off his own cloak, threw it over the beggar's head and swept him indoors. Once in his chambers, Jayendra dismissed the attendants and barred the door. Then he returned to the man and once more scrutinized him with wavering disbelief.

'Brother-in-law! Sire! Is it really you?'

Toramana smiled faintly and nodded.

'You look unwell,' cried Jayendra. 'Here, sit down. Shall I call for a physician?'

Toramana shook his head and gripped the other man's arm.

'My family,' he whispered weakly. 'Have you news of them?'

'Have no worry, sire, they are safe!' Jayendra assured him.

Toramana shook with relief. 'Tell me all.'

'I found them quite by accident. After you were exiled from the capital, King Hiranya kept a close guard on our family… indeed, he still does! Neither my father, I, nor any of our relatives could send out to look for Anjana.

'But quite by chance I found myself at a village where I saw there a group of potters' boys at play. Watching them, it struck me that the leader of the boys was somehow different from the others. He seemed to shine like a lotus in a murky pond. Following their play, I saw also that he showed strength and discernment, treating the boys kindly, yet compelling their obedience.

'When I stepped forward and greeted him gently, he received me with the easy condescension of a king's son. More and more curious, I had the boy take me to visit his home and parents. What unexpected joy it was to find there my own beloved sister!'

Jayendra saw tears in Toramana's eyes and paused.

'I *do* have a son!' whispered the frail king.

'And what a magnificent boy he is, sire,' beamed Jayendra with avuncular pride. 'Anjana, who was fleeing from the king, was sheltered by a potter's family. There she gave birth to the boy and named him Pravarasena. I have since taught him the ways of a prince and he is keen, sire, to right the many wrongs done to you and to his mother.'

'Pravarasena,' Toramana savoured the name, letting it roll off his tongue. The syllables gladdened his heart.

'Tell him,' he cried, 'tell my boy Pravarasena that he must take back the throne. But not immediately. Let him spend the next five years gathering people who will acknowledge and fight alongside him. He must cement his base before he challenges the emperor.'

Jayendra looked puzzled. 'It is you, not he, who will reclaim the throne. And you already have the support of thousands!'

'Look at me, brother,' Toramana smiled wryly, 'I am all done in. My son is safe and fulfilling his destiny, while I have nothing left to give.' Through gritted teeth, he added, 'And when I die, for certain Hiranya will die too!'

Jayendra's objections were quickly hushed. Toramana continued, 'Hiranya has no heirs. Our overlord Emperor Vikramaditya will send a man from his own court to take over this land. What cares he for our lineage so long as he regularly receives tribute? When my son seeks his inheritance, he will therefore be fighting none other than the great Vikramaditya.'

A loud banging interrupted them. 'Uncle, let me in!' came the desperate voice of Pravarasena.

Jayendra unbarred the door and the young man burst through. Almost knocking his uncle out of the way, he ran to the frail body on the couch and dropped to his knees before it. He was just in time to hold his father as Toramana breathed his last. In his palace, Hiranya felt the air leave his lungs. His heart seized, darkness fell over his eyes, and he knew he was dying. His soul fled with that of his twin.

As Toramana had predicted, Emperor Vikramaditya sent a favoured scholar-poet, Maitrigupta, from Ujjain to take the throne in Shrinagari. None of the courtiers dared say a word against this. Pravarasena too did not wish to harm him, for he considered Maitrigupta a weak academician, an unworthy foe.

He wished to pit his might against Vikramaditya, the only ruler he considered an even match. Over five hard years, Pravarasena campaigned across the land, winning the hearts of his people, raising a mighty army and preparing for the long march to the emperor. In the year 19 CE, just as he was about to set out, word reached him that Vikramaditya too had passed away.

The son of Anjana and Toramana thus marched upon Maitrigupta's capital instead. The poet, however, was desolate to hear that Vikramaditya, his master, had died. Whom would he serve now? For whom did he suffer to hold this state? Maitrigupta willingly stepped down and Pravarasena ascended the throne. He ruled for over sixty years as an exceptional warrior king. When Vikramaditya's son was exiled by his enemies, it was Pravarasena who restored him to the throne, thus making a vassal out of the old emperor's heir.

ALEXANDER GETS A GURU

A shout to halt brought Lysimachus out of his meandering thoughts. He raised his arm in command to the phalanx of foot soldiers following him. Before him, the meadow rolled out into the distance, its verdant sweep of grass and wildflowers shaded by billows of low-hung clouds.

It was then that he spotted the naked men.

Lysimachus frowned and rubbed his eyes. Perhaps the long march with the battle-weary army was playing tricks on his eyes.

But no, there they were. A few hundred feet away, the pasture was strewn with a small band of men. Despite the cool wind and the moisture in the monsoon air, they were clad in the merest scraps of loincloth. Many of them had dispensed with clothes entirely.

One of the generals up front beckoned. Lysimachus spurred his horse forwards.

'See you these sages, Lysimachus?' the general gestured to the world at large.

'I see entirely too much of them.' Then the key word struck him. 'Sages? *Sages*, sir?' he cried.

The general harrumphed. 'These may well be the ascetics Alexander has been looking for.'

Lysimachus looked at the spindly brown figures and sniggered. But before his ill-thought words left his lips, the general snapped, 'Rein it in, soldier!'

'Yes, sir!' responded Lysimachus. He considered the men dotting the meadow and remarked, 'They do look remarkably like our philosopher Diogenes.'

'What do you know of Diogenes?'

'When we passed through Corinth, we came upon a man who lived in a barrel. He was old and sagging, hairy and unkempt, and clothed just as completely as these ascetics before us. And rude! He relieved his bowels in public where all could see and smell it! Yet, everyone treated him with respect.'

'As they should so profound a philosopher,' replied the general. 'Why, Alexander too sought him out and asked if he could be of service. Diogenes, who was basking at the time, stretched out his fingers and said, yes, the prince could cease blocking his sun.'

Lysimachus chuckled.

The general continued, 'To one so contemptuous of social values and status, Alexander felt compelled to justify his ambition. The victorious Greeks should dance in India, the conqueror said, and bring our Bacchic revels to its wild tribes.

'And now you see them, Lysimachus. In this place, holy men are even more frugal than Diogenes – for here, they have no need of a wallet. In such a place they do not store up food, since they have it ever fresh and green from the earth; the flowing rivers give them drink and they have fallen leaves and grassy beds to lie upon. "Because of me," Alexander has claimed, "even those faraway sages shall come to know of Diogenes, and he of them."'

'What now, general?' asked Lysimachus. 'Will the king discourse with them? Take them with us?'

'Bring forth the interpreters and form a guard about the king. We will set forth to meet them immediately.'

Lysimachus reined back his horse and did as he was bid.

As he turned the steed, he got an eyeful of the fresh green pasture carpeted by the vast battalions of Alexander's army. The legions stretched up and down the undulating valley and spilled beyond the horizon: row upon row of uniformed foot soldiers, thousand-strong cavalry units and, bringing up the rear, monstrous siege engines, hulking catapults and ingenious bits of military engineering born from the devious mind of Aristotle, Alexander's teacher back home.

Still, for all its fearsome mien, this was an army of little cheer. The conquest of Indian lands in the humid monsoon was taking its toll. The battle with King Puru had been the last straw.

Under lashing sheets of water, the men had forded the mighty Jhelum. Just when drowning seemed the worst they could face, Puru threw at them a never-before-seen monstrosity – the elephant battalion. Trapped behind a river in flood and half blind in the gloom of the downpour, the men fought tusked giants that barrelled down, piercing, trampling, decimating all in their path.

Despite the odds, Alexander's brilliant tactics carried the day and his army prevailed – but only just. In the treaty that followed, Alexander reinstated Puru, making him a tributary king.

Tens of thousands died in the battle. Alexander's own champion horse, Bucephalus, breathed its last from wounds sustained while fighting Puru's elephant. The prince had given him a moving burial and ordered a city built in his name.

Depleted in numbers and morale, the army was now grimly moving south-west. Dissatisfied whispers rippled through the ranks. The leaders held their tongues no better.

Lysimachus had fought heroically in the battle against Puru's armies. Not that his courage had ever been in question. As a young warrior of a noble family, he had begun his career as Alexander's bodyguard. When the prince once condemned a man to a slow, torturous death, Lysimachus had taken pity and smuggled a quick-acting poison to the doomed prisoner.

The act of mercy had sent his prince into a rage. Alexander commanded that his guard be thrown into a pit with a hungry lion. Lysimachus recalled being forced into that vault, its bleak stone walls like firm brackets to the short clause of his life's story. Then, at the darkest end, the bars slowly rose. A slavering maw came into view and behind it, a maddened, starved creature skulked forward. A lion, he realized, or the near skeleton of one.

Before the predator could make its move, Lysimachus pounced towards it. Quick as a snake, his hand darted into the gaping mouth and ripped out its tongue. The beast backed up, roaring in anguish.

And just like that, the battle was over. The pitiful feline quickly bled out and Lysimachus was left alone in the cage, his captors stupefied by the one-act play. When Alexander heard the extraordinary tale, he at once reinstated his bodyguard with full honour and proclaimed him the noblest of Macedonians.

Puru had proved a far more worthy adversary than the lion. The way he had pitted his armies against Alexander's, the sheer strength of his troops and his wily use of weather, spies and natural barriers, all compelled the invaders' awe and respect.

Were the rest of India to prove as treacherous in climate and as ruthless in leadership, could they, would they, survive? It was a troubling doubt that, like malaria and typhoid, ran rampant throughout the Macedonian army.

Lysimachus pushed the grim thoughts aside. Wary of the discontent he saw on the men's faces, he called only his most trusted aides forward. Other batches were gathered by Alexander and soon a detachment of the mightiest Macedonians rode to meet the gymnosophists in their meadow.

Mounted on noble chargers, robes flapping in the breeze, helmets and pikes gleaming even on that grey, sunless day, the conquering titans bore down upon the sages in a flurry of flying mud and grass.

The sages heard the great drumming of hooves. The vibrations had them up and hopping – for they stood up and jumped and stamped their feet. They did this for a minute and then went back to their pursuits, ignoring the looming horde.

Alexander felt a stir of interest. Here was something new. A few feet from the men, he reined in his horse and sent forth his interpreters to question their odd behaviour.

As the interpreters explained their purpose, he watched the ascetics turn to him – some with pity, some more understanding and yet others with a dismissive look. One who seemed more sympathetic among them sent back a reply.

Returning to the king, the interpreters gave him the message from the sage who was called Dandamis:

'King Alexander, a human can possess only as much of the earth as he stands upon. You are human like the rest of us. Only, you are always busy and up to no good, travelling so many miles from your home, a nuisance to yourself and others. Ah, well! Soon, you will be dead, and then you will own just as much of this earth as will suffice to bury you.'

Lysimachus drew in a sharp breath. Knowing first-hand how little it took to set off the prince, he fully expected a pool of gore where the sages now stood. But Alexander was not affronted. Indeed, he had heard many philosophers in his time and held many lofty ideals. He was as moved by Dandamis's words as he had been by Diogenes's.

Yet, he held firm by his own vast ambition and sent the interpreters again to narrate his glories to impress upon these humble men that he was no ordinary man but a demigod, the Son of Ammon-Zeus, and thus had high purpose. He invited Dandamis to debate with him further, promising riches and comforts by way of inducement.

'If you, my lord,' Dandamis sent back in reply, 'are the son of god, why then – so am I. I want nothing from you, for what I have is enough. I perceive, moreover, that the men you lead get no good from their worldwide wandering over land and sea, and that of their many travels there will be no end. I desire nothing that you can give me.'

Lysimachus stood before Onesicritus, narrating the incident with the ascetics.

'Even when Alexander threatened to cut off his head, the sage laughed and refused to join the expedition, saying the prince could take his body, but his soul would remain forever. Such madness!'

'Whatever may have been the cause,' replied Onesicritus, a disciple of Diogenes, 'the Indian philosopher is not wrong. All humans, however dominant, rich or poor, will go down equally to dust one day.'

Lysimachus cracked a nut between his knuckles. 'Death? Dust? Why are all sages so full of gloom and doom? Have you no wish to live with passion, to make a name that will last forever? Thousands of years from now, our king will still be remembered. Who will recall these naked men in the meadow?'

'Who is to say who has more power or is truly eternal?' replied Onesicritus. 'Does not the great king seek out philosophers? Who is to say, in a thousand years, whether the king's way or the philosophers' way will have the better outcome.'

'Certainly, the king is pleased with their odd views,' Lysimachus grudgingly admitted. 'Being, after all, a man of high thought and noble purpose, it is natural.'

He took a turn. 'Onesicritus, it is in his mind to invite the sophists to join his campaign, to explore their wisdom at length and let them meet the great minds of Greece. But they remain stubborn – or free, as they claim. Alexander moves you to his cause and asks you to add to his persuasions; secure him these men as his new spiritual advisers.'

Onesicritus thought the sages were wise to ignore an invitation from a man bent on conquering the world with armies. Yet, upon further exhortation from Lysimachus, he agreed to talk to them. He was curious too, to see these philosophers whose words echoed those of his master and seemed to go much further.

And so it was that Onesicritus, walking through the meadow one day, came face to face with the ascetic Kalanos as he lounged upon smooth stones, lost in deep contemplation.

Onesicritus called out his indolence with sharp words, 'In the old days, the world was as full of barley and wheat as now it is of dust. Fountains flowed, some with water, others with milk or honey, and others yet with wine and olive oil. But being gluttons, for sheer consuming greed, humans fell into arrogance passing all bounds.

'The great god Zeus hated this state of things and destroyed everything! He then gave humans a life of toil. And when they learned self-control and virtues again, then he gave them an abundance of blessings.'

Kalanos turned his gaze to the Greek, winked and replied, 'And yet humans are such creatures, that when abundance came forth, once more they became satisfied and arrogant. And with it, once more came the danger of destruction. Old man, if your king truly wishes to know the virtues, ask him take off his broad-brimmed hat, his sturdy boots and the heavy mantles that separate him from nature. Let him lie bare-skinned upon these rocks and hear the teachings of our wise men.'

As Onesicritus hesitated, Dandamis, who happened to overhear the conversation, rebuked Kalanos.

'Too much censure,' said Dandamis, 'is also a form of arrogance. Why do you not see instead how the king – to whom we have spoken only rough words – has not punished us. Instead, he continues to seek understanding. And this, though he is busy with government and the running of so great an empire and army.'

Upon these words, Kalanos felt his wrong and sought to repent. He therefore agreed to return with

Onesicritus to Alexander's camp and speak directly with the prince.

Alexander was with his generals, poring over a map, when the two returned. He received Kalanos with delight and respect. And to the sage, he showed the large map pointing out the sites that the army would march to.

'What say you, good sage?' he asked. 'As a native of these regions and a man of learning, what is the most efficient way to unite these lands?'

Kalanos picked up the great leather map and laid it on the ground. The parchment began to roll up around the edges. When Kalanos trod on one corner to flatten it, the opposite curled up. No matter which side he pressed down, another would rise up. Then he stood at the centre of the map and placed both feet slightly apart. The chart lay quietly stretched out beneath him.

'Do you choose to spend your time on the borders, great prince,' Kalanos asked, 'or hold sway from its centre?'

The generals who saw this cheered and thumped their seats in approval. They were already of a mind to return to Macedonia.

Thus it was that Alexander was persuaded to leave India and return home. Kalanos accompanied him on the march back and held many conversations with the prince. Most surprisingly, Lysimachus, after witnessing the sage's persuasive powers in the tent, became an eager pupil of Kalanos.

However, the journey took its toll on the aged scholar. He barely survived the desert march through the Makran, where even men half his age passed away from exhaustion. Knowing his time was coming to a close, Kalanos chose to make an end himself.

In the manner of the great ascetics of his time, he had Alexander build him a large funeral pyre. The prince pleaded earnestly with him, but Kalanos had made up his mind. He would die with dignity as was the manner of his sect.

Unable to dissuade him, Alexander then heaped riches upon the sage and sent a glorious battalion in pomp and ceremony to accompany Kalanos to his pyre.

Many generals who wished to bid farewell followed in the wake of this procession. At the pyre, Kalanos gave to the men around him all the gold, silks and many riches that Alexander had granted him. To Lysimachus, he gave his warhorse, a steed of spirited blood that was usually reserved for kings. So Kalanos bade each man goodbye, but not Alexander. Him, Kalanos saluted, saying, 'We shall meet again in Babylon.'

Then, he ascended the pyre and, amid the blare of trumpets and the wails of his friends, sprinkled himself with libation, cut off his hair and lay upon the fire. His unshrinking calm and courage found mention in the books of the greatest chroniclers of his time.

Strangely enough, Kalanos's last words came true. In less than a year, Alexander the Great fell ill in Babylon and passed away. His empire was almost immediately split up between his generals. And none other than Lysimachus became the *basileus* (king) of Thrace, Asia Minor and Macedon.

ACKNOWLEDGEMENTS

This book is the result of nearly four years of reading, research, conversations and writing. I am grateful to my publishers for their patience and support during the entire process: to Vatsala Kaul Banerjee for her thoughtful feedback, thorough checks and unflagging follow-ups, all of which raised this book to another level; and to Nimmy Chacko, whose confidence in the original outline encouraged me to put in the hard work. I would also like to thank Sheeba Bhatnagar for her copy-edits and Anjana Sridharan for bringing the stories to life with her fabulous artwork.

My deepest gratitude to Dr Shashi Tharoor for taking the time, despite his busy schedule, to encourage and appreciate a first-time author. Thank you also to his staff – Mr Padmakumar, Rohit Suresh and John Koshy – for furthering my efforts. I am fortunate to have on my side my cousin Geetha and her husband T.S. Ramesh, whose astute guidance helped me reach all the right people.

The idea for this book germinated from the brusque and tragicomic tales of my grandfather, who took me around Sthanumoorthy Kovil, pointing out grotesque carvings and recounting Brothers Grimm-like stories from a more astonishing and adventurous era. It has been a near-impossible task to capture the atmosphere and enchantment of his idiomatic Tamizh.

My family is my alpha and omega. I am rooted to the ground thanks to my parents, partner, brother and mother-in-law. Without them, my endeavours would have all remained castles in the air. Thank you for being a part of my life.

SV Iyer
Mumbai, 2024